THE MOTHER-IN-LAW

SL HARKER

CHAPTER ONE

Gravel crunches under the weight of the car, and I listen to the popping and scraping as each tiny pebble grinds into the earth. As Mark brings the car around to the circular front drive, I glance out the window. He lets the engine idle a moment then shuts it off. We're here, and I'm not sure I want to be.

I lick my lips and stare up at the house. "It's... really... red." I let out a nervous laugh.

"Makes a bold statement, huh?"

I glance at Mark, whose big hands are planted on the wheel. He's wearing his lazy, vague smile. When I'm in a good mood, I find that smile charming, but when I'm in a bad mood, it's annoying. Right now, I'm stuck somewhere in between, too tired to be fully annoyed but not exactly happy either.

"I was going to say it's more like murder red, but okay." I smile.

Mark's laughter floats through the space between us. He clamps a hand on my neck and kneads the soft skin with his fingers. He always knows exactly when and how to touch me. "Come on, baby. It's not that bad, is it?"

His sharp gray eyes search my face, matching the mist and fog that cloak the house in front of us. This is his mother's house, the house he grew up in. It doesn't harbor this sense of foreboding for him because he's used to it. But I can't help but feel dread crawling through my veins. This is my future, and I'm not sure I want it. I reframe my thoughts. *This is temporary. Our future will be more than this. This is just to get us back on our feet.*

"Jess?" Mark frowns slightly. "Are you okay? Are you having second thoughts? We did both agree—"

"Mark, I'm fine. I am. I'm just tired from the drive. That's all."

I shift my gaze back to the house. The bloodred bricks pop out from the fog, and the white shutters and the bay windows bulge like eyeballs. I try to shake my worries away. Mark's mother has lived here alone since his dad died, and it's clear from the peeling paint on the shutters that she's struggled to keep on top of maintenance. Guilt creeps in. Maybe that's my fault for hogging her son. I shake my head slightly, pushing my worries away.

"Well, I like the butterfly lawn ornaments in the rose garden. The ivy crawling up the side is cozy too," I admit.

Mark pulls me to him and takes my head in his hands. "Everything is going to be okay, baby. You'll love it here. You'll have so much space to move around. My mom will dote on you and wait on you for anything you need. And it's only temporary, right? So we can save up for that house down payment."

"Thanks, but I really don't want anyone doting on me. Maybe you could—"

THE MOTHER-IN-LAW

A piercing wail sounds. I swivel again, peering through the passenger window.

Mark's mother is barreling down the steps, her knobby knees clinking together, her veins like purple rivers under paper-thin skin. Her silver hair cascades down her shoulders. She waves, her face full of glee.

Since I'm an introvert, this kind of emotional abandon makes me wince. But I plaster on a smile and try not to let my discomfort show. My mother-in-law stops in front of my door, yanks it open, and grabs my hand. Her skin is cold, but her energy is warm.

Mark says, "Uh, Mom, just wait a second—"

"Oh, darling, I'm just so excited to see you all!" Catherine exclaims, dragging me out of the seat.

She pulls me into a hug so tight I can't breathe and pats me on the back like I'm a baby in need of a burp. As she pulls away, her hands remain on my arms, and her dark eyes assess me. "You look radiant, Jess. Marriage suits you."

"Thanks, Catherine." I try to match her beaming smile even though her abrupt entry into my personal space makes my pulse run a bit faster.

Mark walks around the side of the car. "What am I? An afterthought?" He opens his arms, and Catherine folds herself into them.

"It's so good to see you again, darling, after such a long time." Catherine presses her face to her son's chest.

"I missed you, too, Mom."

My heart flutters at the endearing way he says it. I feel like I'm intruding on a private moment between mother and son, so I flick my eyes back to the house, where they're drawn to the round attic window. Tilting my head, I stare up at it, trying not to think about Stephen King novels and old haunted houses. For a moment, I think I see a shadow or something move, but then I blink and shake my head.

Mark's voice pulls me out of my thoughts. "Everything okay?" he asks, sliding one hand over my lower back.

"Yeah, it's just…" I point up at the round window. "It's nothing." I laugh it off. "I thought I saw something moving up there."

Catherine's face washes out to the color of dishwater, but she recovers instantly. She gives Mark a smirk as if sharing a private joke.

"Oh, it's just those old windows. They need a good clean! You'll get used to it. I promise." Catherine waves a hand dismissively and links her arm with mine at the elbow to coax me along.

"I've always thought the house might be haunted." Mark chuckles and lifts one of our bags out of the trunk then heaves it over his shoulder.

I gawk at him. "What? You never told me that."

Catherine combs her fingers through the back of my hair. She's really touchy-feely, and I'm not sure I like it, but I don't want to hurt her feelings, so I try not to flinch.

"Mark is just teasing you, dear. Don't listen to him." Catherine gives me a wink.

Her brown eyes bore into him. I always found it strange how Mark's eyes are a steely gray, like rolling storm clouds set over a sea, but Catherine's are a muddy caramel.

"Hey, you can think what you want, but I know what I saw." Mark frowns, and I realize this is a touchy subject for them both.

We walk up the front porch steps.

"What did you see?" I ask.

Catherine rolls her eyes. "Oh, not that ghostly figure in

your bedroom again. Honestly, Mark, it was years ago, and you need to admit you were dreaming."

I stop on the last step and regard my husband, feeling like the wooden boards are going to give out from under me.

This time, Mark takes my hand and strokes my hair. He's looking only at me. "She's right. It was just a bad dream. No one was there."

"But you just said you know what you saw."

"Mark is a prankster. Surely you know that by now," Catherine jokes, giving her son a playful swat on the arm. "Now come on. I'll give you a tour, and you can see that there is nothing to worry about. Then I'll make lunch. I have ripe vegetables fresh from the garden. I can make us a beautiful spring salad. I'm sure you're hungry from the drive."

"That sounds amazing," I say and mean it, but I still look at Mark for reassurance.

He nods and steps into the house, his fingers threading through mine.

I can't quite believe we're living here with his mother. It's not how I expected our first year of marriage to go. But I've met Catherine several times, and she's nice. Okay, maybe sometimes she gives off strange vibes, but it's just because she's eccentric and a little intense. Everything is going to be fine. I'm sure it will.

As long as this place isn't really haunted.

CHAPTER TWO

The plan is to live here for a few months. That's it. We're not going to be here forever. It's just while we get our shit together. Mark works at an insurance firm, and I'm a remote employee for a graphic design company. Money has been tight recently, and Catherine has graciously offered us a room in her spacious house while we save up for our forever home. The house prices just exploded in the small Maine town we want to settle in, and we had to make a choice—either we continue to rent for the foreseeable future, perhaps even after starting a family, or we move in with Catherine and save up. Somehow, Mark convinced me to go with the latter, though part of me wishes we'd moved a few states over to live with my grandparents in New York. Though, it just wasn't practical with their tiny apartment and the fact that Mark's office is based in Portland.

We step over the threshold into the narrow foyer, which is crawling with shadows. The wooden plank floors groan as we move across a narrow patterned rug. A single lamp sits on a table at the end of the cramped space, sending a cone of light up to the ceiling but nowhere else. In the center, a staircase curves at an angle. Black-and-white sketches line the walls.

My gaze lands on a set of family photographs arranged on a table to the left of the staircase. I lift one to examine it more closely. It's also black-and-white. The woman in the picture's dark hair is curled at the ends and hovers just above her shoulders. She's wearing a simple light-colored dress with a belt around the middle to cinch the waistline. Next to her is a man in a dark suit and a fedora. Their posture is stiff, and their fingers lightly touch though are not entwined.

"Those were my late husband's parents."

I jump and nearly drop the photo then quickly return it to its place. "Sorry. I—"

"That's okay, sweetie." Catherine smiles and touches my arm. "This is your home now."

"My grandfather built this house," Mark explains. "The whole place was his project."

"Wow." I crane my neck up the staircase. "What an impressive project!"

Catherine shrugs. "Maybe at the time, but I hate to admit I've let things go a little recently."

"Oh, not at all," I gush. "It's a beautiful home. And Mark can touch things up if you like."

Mark rolls his eyes slightly, as if saying, "Sure I will."

I give him a quick jab with my elbow.

"Of course, Mom," Mark says. "I'll get Dad's tools out at the weekend and make a start."

"That's kind of you both. Thank you." Catherine motions for us to follow her upstairs. "I'll show you to your room."

The hallway upstairs is not as narrow as the foyer but is equally dark. Mark carries one of our suitcases, following Catherine, until we reach the last door. Her skinny fingers turn an antique doorknob.

This room, unlike the others downstairs, is bathed in light. The afternoon sun splashes across the walls, illuminating the dust still lingering in the air. I smile broadly at the Pepto Bismol–colored wallpaper in an attempt to hide my shock. Next to me, Mark clears his throat as though holding in his own reaction. I allow my gaze to travel over to the furniture. The mahogany four-poster bed is certainly big enough for us both. Ornately carved wood posts lead up to the purple canopy above. I've never known a room to be equal parts romantic and eerie before. This place certainly breaks the mold.

Catherine clamps her slender hands together. "I'll leave you two to get settled. There's an en suite bathroom. That's why I chose it for you. After you wash up, come downstairs, and I'll have that delicious spring salad waiting for you."

As soon as I hear her footsteps wandering back down the hall toward the stairs, I turn to Mark. "This isn't the room where you saw the ghost, is it?"

Mark's lighthearted chuckle and the glint in his eyes are enough to slow my rampant pulse. When he pulls me to him, I press my head against the safety of his hard chest. He strokes my back with the heels of his palms, something he often does to soothe me.

He kisses the part in my hair and, in a gentle voice, says, "Baby, don't worry about it. If it wasn't safe, I wouldn't have brought you here." He continues stroking my hair as I try to relax. "Besides, I can't wait to have sex in the bed where my mother was born."

I pull away from him, horrified.

Mark's eyes crinkle, and he leans forward, slapping his knees. "Your face! My mother wasn't born here. My father's father built the house, remember?"

I let out a sigh of relief. "Okay, you're joking, but I bet

someone was born in this bed." I grimace. "Or at least conceived. Do you think the mattress has been updated recently?"

Mark sits down on the end of the bed and reaches for my hand. "Sure." He pulls me closer, and in my head, I think of the conversation we had a few weeks before coming here, the one about how we didn't want to wait to have children.

Soon, I'm lost in the gray of his eyes as he leans in and draws our lips together. I have no choice but to believe him and dive headfirst into this new adventure.

CHAPTER THREE

We spend the day unpacking and settling into the room. Catherine has obviously tidied the bedroom and cleaned the bathroom, but dust seems to have infiltrated every corner of each room. I chase cobwebs from the deepest, darkest crevices.

Catherine is nothing but sweet, offering to help us organize our clothes several times. Her spring salad is as lovely as she described. Then later in the day, she makes a beef casserole for our evening meal. By the time we collapse into bed, we're too pooped to think about the conversation we had about making babies. But I haven't started checking my cycle yet, so I don't mind.

Mark is asleep within seconds—as he always is—but I find it harder to drift off. Every time my eyes droop, I think about the attic window and the flash of movement. *It was nothing. A shadow. Swirling dust. Maybe a bird made its way in.* Yet part of me wonders what Mark saw when he was a child. I know my husband, and he isn't a fantasist. He doesn't believe in ghosts, and no one would call him particularly spiritual. He's a numbers guy, which is one of the things I love about him. I'm the creative one who loves books and movies and escapism. Mark keeps me grounded.

I can't imagine him making up such a strange thing or mistaking a dream for reality, even as a child. But then again, we are all different as children. I refused to wear dresses for my eighth year on this earth because I decided denim shorts looked more grown-up.

My poor mother.

The old house groans and creaks. At one point, I think I hear footsteps, then the house grows silent again. I browse my phone, scrolling through Instagram stories until my eyes droop.

Then I wake with a kiss on my forehead.

"Hey," Mark says. He's dressed and ready for work. "You looked so peaceful I didn't want to wake you. But it's almost eight."

I groan. I'm not a morning person at the best of times, but after a terrible night's sleep, I'm pretty grouchy precaffeine. "Okay, are you leaving?"

He nods. "Yeah. I'm running a little late, actually. Are you okay?"

"Sure. Is your mom up yet?"

"She's in the kitchen."

"Okay. Have a great day, sweetie."

We kiss, and he disappears from the room.

Normally, I'd make breakfast in my PJs, but I decide to shower and get ready first. I put on a pair of jeans and an oversized sweatshirt. Judging by the chill last night, I know this is a cold house. Then I make my way downstairs.

"Morning!" Catherine says. "I made coffee."

"You're a lifesaver. Thanks." I smile and grab the pot.

"Mark told me you're not much of a morning person. I'm afraid I'm up with the rooster." She chuckles. "Still, at least there'll always be hot coffee for you. Oh, and I made pancakes. Mark ate all the bacon, though."

"That's okay. I can't eat before lunch. It upsets my stomach."

"Oh. Sorry." She starts fussing around, picking up dirty plates and taking them to the sink. "I wish Mark had told me. I wouldn't have made all this. Oh, what a silly fool I am."

"I'm so sorry," I say, mortified by how upset she sounds. "I should have mentioned it yesterday at dinner."

"Not at all. You're a guest. I like to make my guests welcome in my house. I can reheat these for Mark tomorrow." She grabs a Tupperware box from a cupboard.

I want to tell her that Mark is thirty years old now and can make his own damn breakfast, but I hold my tongue. "Is there anything I can help you with before I get to work?"

She pauses. "I thought you worked from home, dear."

"I do. But I still have to log on to my laptop before nine. I have a Zoom call with a client."

"Oh," she says. "I see. Well, no, not really. I can clean this up."

I eye the dirty plate, thinking that Mark should have washed it before he left. But I'm sure his mother insisted she do it herself. She is excited to have us here. Maybe she'll calm down and stop coddling us once we're settled in.

It's almost nine, so I reluctantly leave her to it, settling into Mark's father's office. We talked about it last night, and Catherine was excited for me to work in here. I take in the large green leather chair and the mahogany desk. The place smells like tobacco and whisky, like how I imagine a boardroom at a corporation smells, with all that testosterone emanating from important shareholders. This is quite the office.

I settle into the chair, lean back, and get ready for the

Zoom meeting. Maybe things won't be so bad. At least my clients are going to think I work somewhere fancy, and I can treat myself to that luxurious croissant-scented candle to chase away the smell of tobacco.

The meeting goes well. I then make a list of the tasks I want to accomplish. About an hour in, I get a phone call from a prospective client and take them through what I offer in terms of service. I'm partway through the interview when the office doors swing open and a burst of cold air rushes in. I glance up and watch an uninvited Catherine strut into the room. She's holding a white porcelain mug and stops in front of the desk and sets it beside me.

"Freshly brewed coffee just the way you like it, a tablespoon of sugar and a splash of vanilla cream."

I give her as polite a smile as I can manage and gesture to the laptop. "Thanks," I mouth. "I'm just on a call."

Catherine nods, but instead of turning to leave, she parks herself in the seat across from my desk, crosses her legs, and folds her slender fingers over her knees.

I try not to appear flustered and quickly revert my gaze to my laptop screen, but her presence is impossible to ignore and irritatingly distracting.

"Okay, got it," I say. "But maybe you could send me a few examples via email?"

The room feels impossibly hot. Perspiration breaks out across my nose as I end the call even though we had more to discuss.

"Hey, Catherine," I say. "Can I do something for you?"

Catherine sighs. "I just thought you might want some company."

"That's kind of you, but I'm really busy right now. That was a client, actually, and I'm working under some tight deadlines at the moment."

Catherine frowns, gesturing to the coffee. "You should drink that before it gets cold."

"Thank you. I will."

A silence fills the space between us, becoming denser the longer it goes on.

Finally, Catherine stands. "I'll have lunch ready in an hour. Perhaps you'd like to take a break then and join me on the patio in the backyard?"

"I'd like that. Thank you."

She leaves, closing the door behind her. I exhale a heavy breath and lean back in my chair, staring unfocused at my laptop screen. Catherine zapped my concentration. I knead the nape of my neck to ease some of the tension.

I remind myself that Catherine is just trying to be accommodating to make me feel welcome in her home. Maybe I'm not giving her the credit she deserves.

Finally, I immerse myself back into my work, and before the hour is up, I shut my laptop and head to the kitchen, hoping to repair any damage I may have done to Catherine's ego.

"Need any help with preparing lunch?" I ask.

Catherine is chopping cucumbers. She glances at me over her shoulder. "Sure. Can you give me a hand and slice the bread?"

"It smells heavenly in here."

Catherine's cheeks turn rosy with pride. "That's the loaf of French bread I made this morning."

My stomach grumbles with a sudden pang of hunger. "Yum."

A few minutes later, we sit down under the ivy-strewn awning outside to eat. The ice clinks in our lemonade glasses. The warm sun beats down on our shoulders, and the breeze tickles our cheeks. Birds chirp in the tree branches. The cobalt sky brings out the vibrancy of the lush green grass. It's a beautiful day.

"Mark used to run laps around the perimeter of the property," Catherine mentions between bites, dabbing her cloth napkin at the edges of her lips.

"Oh yeah?" I perk up at a story about my husband when he was younger.

Catherine gazes out at the lawn wistfully. "He always had so much energy. He was so impulsive."

I laugh. "He's still those things."

Catherine gives me a funny look then settles back into her sandwich.

"Of course, I love his sense of adventure," I add quickly. "He keeps life interesting."

Her eyes light up when I say that. "He sure seems to be fond of you."

Warmth flutters across my face, and I nod, taking a sip of my ice-cold lemonade to quelch the heat spreading through me.

"These six months married to him have been some of the best of my life," I add.

In a sudden flash of vulnerability, I feel the need to be open with Catherine. Maybe it's the affectionate way she's looking at me or the sentimental story she shared about Mark. Either way, my soft interior wants to surface, buttered up by Catherine's maternal presence.

"It was hard losing my parents so young." I pause a moment and reach for Catherine's hand on the table and give it a squeeze, surprising myself. "I just want you to know how much I appreciate your kindness and hospitality. I don't have a mother anymore to share things with and talk to, so it's nice to get to be here, spending time with you."

Catherine returns the squeeze to my hand, and her brown

eyes show flecks of caramel that glint in the sun. "Darling, you can share anything with me anytime. I'm here for you. It's an honor for you to say such nice things to me. I'm grateful you and Mark are here. It's a big house, and it can get lonely. It's refreshing to hear other voices."

She stands to gather our plates and glasses, but I stop her. "Let me clean up for you."

"Oh, I don't mind a bit." She places her hand on my arm, coaxing me back to my seat. "Just enjoy the sunshine."

"Sorry." I chuckle. "I've been on my own for a long time, and I'm used to it. I guess I've had to learn to be self-sufficient, and it's a hard habit to break."

That is one difference between Mark and me. He doesn't mind a bit if someone else wants to do something for him, but he's pretty good about returning favors.

Catherine pats my shoulder the way only a mother could. "Don't worry about it. Everybody deserves a little pampering every now and then."

CHAPTER FOUR

The lunch with Catherine manages to put my mind at ease, and the next few days go smoothly. Mark gets up for work early each morning. Catherine makes me coffee, and we usually lunch together. Sometimes, she tells me stories about Mark. Other times, we stay inside the house and she introduces me to her favorite soaps.

"Mark and I watched this show all through summer," she says, the ice in her tea tinkling against the glass. "We'd spend the whole summer together, even when he was a teenager. He loved spending time with me." She sips her drink and smiles.

"It's nice how close you are," I say, but I can't help wondering about Mark's friends. *Didn't he go to camp? Or play with local school friends?* Now that I think about it, Mark never mentioned his summers, not even when I told him about the volleyball camp I went to during sixth grade, right before my parents had their accident.

In the evenings, Catherine usually cooks, and I drag Mark off his ass to clear up. Then we drink a little wine in the sitting room before heading to bed.

It's almost midnight. Mark and I have just finished

making love for the third time since arriving at the estate, and I lay cuddled in his arms, our bodies still sweaty, intertwined, our heartbeats still pounding, his hands threaded through my hair. I trace my nails across his chest, fatigue coiling around me.

"I'm having fun here," I admit.

His fingers brush across my arm. "I'm happy to hear it, baby."

"I'm getting closer to your mom."

"She's not driving you nuts yet?"

I laugh. "She means well."

"I suppose that's a yes, then. You can tell her to back off."

"I wouldn't dare. Besides, I don't mind it. Unless I'm on the phone with a client or something. I think she's just lonely and trying to make up for lost time in not being around other people for so long."

"It's reassuring that you are getting along." He pauses and takes a deep breath, and I notice his heart kick up a notch against my ear. "Which leads me to what I need to talk about with you next."

I push off his chest and prop myself up on one elbow, studying him. He licks his lips, and his pupils dilate. He's nervous about something.

"What's going on?" My stomach clenches.

"You have been so supportive of my career, baby." He eases me in, threading the needle. I admire his effort.

"But?"

He smiles, but it doesn't reach his eyes. "How did you know I hadn't gotten to the punch line yet?"

"Because I don't feel punched by it," I try to joke, but my stomach is still tapping with butterflies.

"A senior manager on my team has just dropped out of a major project we were working on."

"Okay..."

Mark finally meets my gaze. "This has opened an opportunity for me. Sort of a good-news, bad-news situation."

"Mark, you know I hate suspense. Just spit it out already."

"I have to leave for Japan." He blurts all the words out in one fluid motion, and they all fall out of his mouth in one tangled mess.

"For... how long?"

"Six to eight weeks, depending on how things go."

The walls start to close in on me. Any bit of the euphoria I'd been experiencing post sex has now evaporated. I sit up, tugging up the sheets to cover my naked chest.

"*What?* What am I supposed to do?"

"You can stay here. Like you said, you and Mom are getting on really well. Please don't be upset." He strokes my cheek, but I turn my head away. His hand falls limply to the mattress, and his brow knits.

"We've only been here a week, Mark, and now you're leaving?"

"I'm sorry, baby. I don't know what else to do. I have to take this job, or else I might be pushed out altogether."

"Have you told your mother yet?"

"Of course not. You're the first person I was going to tell... always. I only just found out this afternoon."

"And you wait until after we fuck to tell me?"

His eyes narrow, storm clouds rolling in them. "Jess, please, keep your voice down."

"You didn't tell me to be quiet a few minutes ago," I bite back.

His face softens. "I'm not trying to upset you."

I lay my head on the pillow and sigh, watching the ceiling fan blades whirl in a circle. Then I turn my head and look at him. His gray eyes are crackling with sadness.

"Sorry," I mutter. "It's just such a shock. We've only been married six months. And now we're living with your mother. And we're trying for a baby. And you're... *leaving*." I shake my head, dumbfounded. This is all happening too fast.

"I get it. But this is a great opportunity. If I go, it means we can save up for the house in half the time. It's going to work out for the best. I promise." He wraps his arms around me and holds me close until I feel secure enough to close my eyes and drift off into a fretful sleep.

CHAPTER FIVE

CATHERINE AND I ARE AT THE TOP OF THE ATTIC STAIRS. SHE NEEDS help clearing out some old junk, and I need a distraction from the fact that Mark will be going away soon. And he hasn't told his mother yet. Catherine pulls a white string, and a bulb above us illuminates. Dust collects on every windowsill and cabinet surface, and little orbs of it float around the space as we move through the piles of junk.

A tingle whispers across the back of my neck and sends a chill down my spine. I shudder and wrap my arms around my chest, following Catherine as she traipses, her muscle memory familiar with the constricted space.

We maneuver through a maze of trunks and dressers, piles of clothes, old toys, and ornaments. I bend at the peaked angles where we can't stand up straight.

"Ah-ha!" Catherine exclaims.

When I turn, I find her crouched in a dark corner. Again, a chill travels across the nape of my neck. The onset is so abrupt that it snatches all my focus, and I spin around, expecting someone to be standing there.

"Jess?"

"Huh?" I slowly turn around again, blinking into Catherine's face. She's standing now, several paces away from me.

"Everything all right?" she asks. Her voice is too melodic, like it's dripping honey.

"Yeah, I, uh—I just... thought I felt something behind me. Moving."

I watch Catherine's face carefully, but she's as poised as always. I still don't understand how she can seem so well put together all the time.

"The house is drafty, dear. Remember I told you this?"

I lick my lips and shift my weight, clamping my hands together to keep them from shaking.

"Right. Yes. I remember."

I glance at the cone of darkness behind her. She's pulled open a large trunk, and a handle is sticking out from it.

She juts a finger over her shoulder, smiling, but her eyes are still focused on me. "I found the suitcases for Mark."

"Great." As if suddenly remembering how to move, my legs coax me forward, and I start lifting the suitcases from the trunk to help her.

I start descending the attic stairs in front of Catherine. They are very steep and narrow, making it challenging to lug the heavy suitcase. It's a rolling one, so I try to just bump it along on my way down, but once I get halfway, I lose my footing on the wide slots of the attic step, and my knee buckles. I try to brace myself on the wall, as there's no railing for me to grab. I let out a gasp, and the rest happens so fast it's somehow almost as if it's happening in slow motion.

After a crack then a snap, I'm tumbling. I land palms down on the hardwood floor of the hallway. A sharp, excruciating pain throbs from my ankle and radiates all the way up my leg, where it tangles around my hips.

I try to stand, but my ankle screams in protest, and I let out a yelp of agony.

Catherine shuffles down the remaining steps and kneels before me. Her eyes are wide and frightened. She clamps a hand on my hip and, with a grunt, helps bring me to a sitting position.

"Oh, darling!" She shakes her head as if unprepared to deliver bad news. "It's definitely not supposed to be bent that way."

"What?" I shriek, panic cleaving me. My eyes instinctively wander downward, and my stomach lurches when I see my ankle bone bent at the wrong angle.

"Oh my god."

"It's all right. We'll get you to a hospital. I'll call Mark now and tell him to come home."

I wince again, the pain pulsing through my foot and shin. The skin around my ankle is already starting to swell and bruise.

"Then I'll get some ice. All right? Are you okay here?"

I nod, too shocked to speak. The pain continues to radiate through my ankle and leg, and with it brings waves of nausea. I tip my head forward, watching beads of sweat drip onto the carpet. From downstairs comes Catherine's voice on the phone, followed by her rushing around the house. Then a few moments later, she returns with a bag of ice.

"Here, sweetheart." She passes me the bag, and I press it gently to the hurt ankle.

"He's on his way," she says, hooking an arm over my shoulder. "Don't worry. Everything is going to be okay. Mommy's here."

* * *

Six hours later, the three of us return home with Chinese takeout. It's been a long day. My ankle is throbbing, even with the painkillers, and I've been given a boot to wear. Catherine is still as pale as the moment she saw my injury. Mark keeps running his hands through his hair and grimacing. I don't have a lot of appetite, but I manage a few bites after Catherine arranges the food on the table.

"Don't worry," she says. "You'll be back on your feet in no time. And I'm going to take good care of you until then."

"We both will," Mark says, grasping my hand. "I'm so sorry I wasn't here when it happened."

No, he wasn't here because he was at work. And I should have been working, too, but I couldn't say no to Catherine when she needed help, because I feel guilty about our staying here. It's only going to get worse once he goes to Japan.

Later, when we're alone, I prop myself on the edge of the bed to pull on my PJs. Mark helps me slide out of my boot, revealing the cast underneath. The doctor said I'd need the cast for four weeks and the boot for another two after that to help the bone set properly.

"You really cracked it like an egg," the doctor tried to joke, but by that time, I was too tired and in pain to manage more than a sliver of a smile for his benefit.

"I can't believe your mom lives all the way out here by herself," I say as I slide on my bottom to my pillow, trying not to move my foot too much.

"She's used to it," Mark says then heads to the bathroom to brush his teeth and wash up for bed.

"Yeah, but it doesn't seem very safe. The city is so far."

Mark leans his head out of the bathroom. He's grinning with the toothbrush in his mouth, a twinkle in his gray eyes. "You don't have to tell me that. I commute every day."

I rub my knee and tuck the sheets up to my waist.

The faucet runs a moment, and Mark emerges after, patting his mouth with a hand towel. His features are suddenly stoic. "I don't have to go to Japan, Jess."

I sit up straight and immediately start shaking my head. "Yes, you do."

He sits on the edge of the bed and places a hand tenderly on my thigh, above the sheet. "I can't leave you like this."

"It's even more reason to leave," I argue.

Mark quirks an eyebrow.

"Think about it. I have your mom here to help me manage until my foot heals. You are on track to make partner. That's more important right now. The faster that happens, the faster we can get our own house, one closer to the city."

Mark gazes at his lap, nodding, before flicking his eyes back to me. "You're sure?"

"I am not going to be responsible for blowing this opportunity for you."

"Only I can do that myself. Is that what you're saying?" he jokes.

I playfully swat his arm. "Get in bed. I've had a long day. I want to go to sleep."

Mark switches off the nightstand light and slides into bed beside me. I feel like we're two pieces of a puzzle clicking into place perfectly.

"I'm going to miss you so much," I whisper in the dark. "Go kick some ass and come back to me a few rungs up the corporate ladder."

"Yes, ma'am." Mark laughs, his breath tickling the back of my ear.

I fall asleep with his hands in my hair, holding on to the memory so I can go back to it when there is nothing but an empty spot in the bed next to me.

CHAPTER SIX

As a fire crackles, Catherine and I sit on the couch. I can't pull my eyes away from the dancing orange flames.

We're having a wine-and-pizza night. She turned on a black-and-white movie from the forties that I can't concentrate on. My eyes keep drifting back to those flames.

Finally, Catherine notices and hits the pause button. "Is everything all right, Jess?"

"Sorry," I say and rub my forehead, feeling the beginning of a headache blossoming between my temples. "I just miss Mark."

I hadn't gone to the airport because of my boot. Instead, I'd spent the day in bed with my ankle resting on several pillows and cried as he closed the bedroom door. *Six, possibly eight, weeks. I can't bear it.*

Catherine gives me a sympathetic smile. "It's only the first day. It will get easier. I promise." She laughs. "My son isn't *that* great. He snores and doesn't load the dishwasher properly."

I sink my shoulders into the cushions and sigh. "He is terrible at stacking the dishes."

Catherine laughs and takes a sip from her glass, looking at me above the rim. "Dishwasher skills aside, he's a wonderful husband to you. So caring and loving. I'm proud of him." She looks down, something sad washing through her caramel eyes. "I guess that means I must have done something right."

I lean forward. "If he didn't love you immensely, he wouldn't have agreed to move here or leave me here. He trusts you, and so do I."

Catherine's eyes are wet when she lifts them and looks at me. "It means a lot that you would say that to me, Jess."

"Well, I do mean it." I lean back again. "And you deserve the company. You've lived alone here for too long. It's not healthy."

Catherine rolls her eyes. "Tell me about it."

I chew on the inside of my cheek, wanting to ask a question but knowing I'll need to choose my words carefully and be sensitive about the delivery.

"How many years has it been since Mark's father died? He doesn't really talk about him much."

"He was quite young when his father passed away," Catherine says, rubbing her arm. "It was fast. From the time he was diagnosed with pancreatic cancer to the time he died, it was only five weeks."

"Wow. I'm so sorry."

Catherine's face is blank as she shrugs. "Nothing could be done. I've accepted it."

"It must have been hard, trying to navigate a world where you just lost your husband and need to raise a child on your own."

Smiling, Catherine says, "Well, Mark certainly kept me on my toes. He was full of life and wanted to play every sport." She chuckles. "Soccer was his favorite. I remember he wanted to have a soccer-themed birthday party when he was nine. I made him a cake shaped like a soccer ball, but the icing was sort of lopsided and gloppy. I might have a picture of it in one of the albums."

"I'd love to see that. I'm sure it tasted great, though. I must admit I've become a little spoiled by your cooking. I don't know what I'm going to do when it's just Mark and me."

Catherine's eyes twinkle. "I can teach you my favorite recipes."

"That would be amazing. Can we look at the old photos if they're easy for you to find?"

"Really?"

"Sure. Who doesn't love reminiscing as they go through old photo albums? Plus, it will give me something to tease Mark about, looking at his baby pictures while he's not here."

Catherine's eyes light up with delight, and she stands then shuffles to an armoire, where she opens a drawer and pulls out a couple of photo albums. "Here. Start with these."

"Perfect."

She plops down next to me, picks up her wineglass again, and clinks it against mine. "Ready to dig in?"

"Couldn't be more excited." I grin and bring my wineglass to my lips.

Catherine sets the album on her lap, opening it. The first several pictures are of Catherine and her husband on their wedding day.

The photos are sepia, aged but timeless. Catherine is a little more filled out in the pictures than she is now but still with a slender figure. She's wearing a simple white silk dress with a veil that floats to the floor. She's beaming, a young woman with the promise of a bright future gleaming in the hope in her eyes.

"That's Nicholas." She points at her husband, who is

holding up a champagne flute. He's wearing a tuxedo, his flaxen hair slicked back, and he's impeccably groomed—clean shaven, with straight white teeth.

I study the picture and realize that Catherine's hair is light-colored too. Mark has dark hair, but neither of his parents did.

Before I can ask about that, Catherine says, "Our wedding was one of the rare occasions when Nicholas drank."

"Oh yeah?"

Catherine gazes at the picture of her husband with a solemn expression, as if she suddenly regrets this impromptu stroll down memory lane. "He was a judge, the youngest and the most prestigious in our county. Everyone knew him. He had a distinguished reputation to uphold in our community. He was well respected, but it came with its fair share of challenges."

"Like what?" As soon as I say it, I let out a tiny gasp, realizing too late the boldness of my question. "I'm so sorry. I don't mean to pry. I just became really engaged in the story."

If Catherine is perturbed by my question, she doesn't show it. Her poise is intact, as always.

"Nicholas ruled the house with an iron fist. I don't mean that literally, of course. He was never physically abusive or anything. It's just... well... he was a man of law and order. He expected the same rules to apply in his home as they did at work. The line between work and family was not defined for Nicholas." She pauses, her lashes fluttering toward her lap. "Sometimes, I felt like I played second fiddle to it all."

"What do you mean?"

"I didn't have much of a voice," Catherine says, still looking at her lap.

I'm surprised she's opening up to me about something so personal. I put my hand on her back to show my support.

"He would shrug me off a lot of the time. It put a strain on our marriage."

"Was Mark tuned in to all that?"

"Oh no." Catherine shakes her head. "He was too young to really understand it."

"Do you think you would have stayed in the marriage if he hadn't died?"

Catherine ponders this. "That's a good question. I'm not sure. We were both raised in conservative, old-fashioned families. As a result, we both had a traditional mindset on marriage. I would probably have stuck it out and tried to make it work. Tried to keep the peace."

I think about this man who—from the sound of it—dominated and controlled his household. Catherine's priorities made her put her husband above herself. The thought makes me sad, and I'm grateful I'm not in a situation like that with Mark.

"Well, you did a truly remarkable job of raising Mark to be a compassionate husband," I tell her. "He's incredible when it comes to understanding my needs and following through with them."

"I'm grateful to hear it, dear." Catherine pats my thigh.

She closes the book with a sense of finality and sets it aside as if she's ready to move on from that conversation. I'll respect her wishes and let it go too. I'm surprised she told me as much as she did.

"I'm happy you feel comfortable enough around me to share things like that."

Catherine's eyes burn into mine. "Of course, dear. You're family. Mark loves you, which means I do too. I never got to have a daughter. You're the closest I'll ever come to it, and I don't want anything to destroy that."

My heart swells at that moment, and I reach out to hug her. Her body is warm and slightly frail.

She pulls away, takes a deep breath, and blots the corners of her eyes with her thumb before opening the second photo album. "Now, shall we find that soccer cake picture?"

I laugh. "Sounds good to me."

As Catherine begins going through each picture of Mark as a little kid, I study her, transfixed by the deep-rooted sadness behind her eyes poking through, even though it seems like she's straining to shove it back.

I get the sudden sense that there's something she's not telling me, that there's more to this story, more to her background with her husband and perhaps even to his death—perhaps even with Mark.

Mark hasn't let on that there were any domestic issues in his household while he was growing up, but then again, perhaps Catherine is being honest. Maybe Mark really was too little to be aware of anything amiss with his parents. I'll have to thread that needle very carefully with both Mark and his mother. For now, Catherine doesn't seem inclined to share any more about it.

CHAPTER SEVEN

I pull the second pant leg over my boot and lift my shirt over my head. Then I hear the doorknob twist, and my heart skips a beat. Instinctively, I cover my chest with my arms and reach for the shirt I just abandoned in a heap on the floor, then I hop as best as I can with a boot on my foot to duck behind the bed.

Catherine sidles into my bedroom, smiling. "Hello, dear."

"Catherine," I say through a breath. "What the hell are you doing?"

She stops dead in her tracks, and the light in her eyes instantly dies, like a bulb being switched off. Her lips pinch together, puckering the skin around her mouth. Instead of covering her eyes and turning around, apologizing, she stands there staring. "Excuse me?" Her usually melodic voice is a sour bark.

"Sorry," I blurt, though a part of me is wondering why I'm the one apologizing. "I didn't mean to snap at you like that. It's just, well, you startled me. That's all. I wish you'd knocked before you came in. I was changing." The statement is as obvious as the quake in my voice.

I watch Catherine's expression as it changes from outrage to sweetness. She shrugs innocently, staring at my head, the only part of my body poking above the bed.

"Oh, come on, Jess. Don't be a prude. I've seen a naked woman's body before. I have one of my own, you know." Her pursed lips curve into a smile.

My heart continues jumping around in my chest, and I'm more defensive than I mean to sound when I say, "Sorry, but I'm just not comfortable expressing myself that way."

"It's not about expressing yourself," Catherine says, shrugging again. "It's just us here. I'm not a nudist or anything. I just figured it was bound to happen eventually. I'm not shaming you." Her caramel eyes burn into mine.

Heat explodes across my face, and in that moment, my self-confidence fractures. I yank the shirt back over my head to keep her from seeing the redness on my face.

I start, "Look, Catherine, I think it might be time to set some boundaries—"

She scoffs. "Come on, Jess. You're my daughter."

I'm not sure what to make of that. It's sweet of her to think of me as a daughter, but she didn't raise me. Even Gran knocks on my bedroom door before she comes in.

"That's a really nice thing to say. I... I think of you as a mother figure too. But I would really like it if you would knock before coming in next time." My voice is still breathless. *What I'd give for Mark to be here right now.* I feel like I need support. Catherine just doesn't seem to be backing down.

"It's not that big of a deal, Jess," she continues. "You're not a victim here. I'm trying to help you. I came in here to see if you needed help bathing yourself because you're hindered by the boot. That's all. I just wanted to help. But if you don't want my help..." She stares at me, a trace of cunning in her eyes, really slathering on that guilt.

"Oh," I say. "Well... no, that's fine. I can manage."

Catherine gives one jerk of her chin and swivels on a heel. "Well, you know where to find me if you change your mind."

She closes the door, not quite a slam but not gently either.

I shake my head and hobble to the bathroom, where I close and lock the door. Then I shut the toilet lid and sit down, my pulse rushing through my ears.

After pressing Mark's number, I listen to the phone ring three times before he picks up. The familiar breeziness to his voice instantly calms me down.

"Hey."

"Hey, baby," Mark says. "How's it going?"

I picture him sitting at his desk, the morning sun like silver beaming across it. Maybe a little dust has collected on a bookshelf behind him or on the mini blinds on his office windows.

I picture his eccentric socks. He loves to wear wacky colors like purple, pink, red, or green. You can only see them if he props his legs up on the desk. I imagine his perfectly polished shoes, which are shiny to the point of appearing almost lacquered, his neatly groomed dark hair a reflection of the same. I picture his mischievous grin and the gray October sky that lives in his eyes.

He probably has a mug of coffee on his desk, too, in his favorite cup from college, which has been filled with almost every consumable liquid, piping hot, steam rising from it before he takes the first sip. I miss him so much in that moment that it's like a physical, stabbing pain.

"I need to talk to you about something. Do you have a sec?"

"For you, baby?" he asks in that dreamy voice that makes me feel like I'm looking up from just beneath the surface of water. "I have all the seconds in the world."

I roll my eyes. "You can layer on the sweetness all you want, but you're still several continents away."

"We can pretend I'm not."

"Well, as much as I love a good game, right now, I need to talk to you about something important."

His frisky demeanor erases itself when he speaks again. "What's wrong?"

"Nothing's... wrong. Not really." I frown and pick at a piece of lint stuck to my knee from where I'd been kneeling on the floor.

"Jess..." His sigh breaks me because he is a problem solver. I know it's hard for him to be so far away from me, where he's less able to find solutions.

"Your mom and I just had our first little spat."

"What about?"

"She walked in while I was changing. I was naked."

"I'm jealous."

"It's not funny, Mark."

"Okay, okay. You're right. I'm sorry. I'm sure she didn't mean it."

"She didn't mean to walk into my bedroom while the door was closed?"

"Boundaries have always been a little murky with Mom," he says.

"Yeah, I'm getting that." He sounds too relaxed, making me feel prickly with irritation.

"Mom has her quirks. I'm sure you're starting to realize that now."

"I'm learning. She offered to *bathe* me, Mark. *Bathe* me."

"Honey, try not to get too upset over it. It's just the way she is. She doesn't know any better. She used to make herself a bubble bath and call me in to talk to her at the end of the day and keep her company."

"Well, that's not too odd if you were a little kid," I say.

"Yeah, she kinda kept doing it while I was a teen too."

"You're joking, right?"

Mark's laughter floats through the phone, but I find this conversation anything but amusing.

"Mark, that's disturbing."

"It really wasn't like that. She'd just ask me what I did at school, what I learned, who I played with. Those kinds of things. I couldn't see her body. It was covered by the bubbles or from whatever color she used as a bath bomb."

"You're not going to convince me that this isn't weird. By the way, I respectfully declined the offer to be bathed by your mother."

"And there's nothing wrong with that. She's just not bothered by nudity as much as normal people are."

"It gave me the ick. Big-time," I say.

He laughs. "Yeah, I'm getting that vibe. Look, just tell her how you feel. She loves you. She'll be fine. Ah shit. I've got to go. My work phone is ringing. I love you, and I miss you like hell."

"I love you too," I say, smiling.

"Good night."

"And good morning to you."

CHAPTER EIGHT

When we hang up, I start running a bath, the sound of the water making me antsy. I wish I could hear what Catherine is doing around the house. *Is she brooding somewhere? Is she getting on with her night?*

After my bath, I decide to grab a glass of water, so I hobble down the stairs with my damp hair. About halfway down, I hear Catherine talking, so I follow the sound of her voice to the kitchen. I could go back upstairs, or I could speak to her again now. If I do go back upstairs, I run the risk of letting this argument fester. So I continue around the corner into the kitchen.

"Oh, that sounds lovely," she says into the phone. "I absolutely can't wait!"

She lets out a giggle that sounds more like a teenage girl's then hangs up. When she turns to see me in the doorway, her eyes widen.

"Oh, hello," she says. "That was just my friend Kathleen."

I smile. "Catherine and Kathleen. That's a tongue twister."

Catherine's smile is sincere with a hint of guilt. "I don't

suppose you heard our conversation about a spa weekend away?"

She's behaving like a teenager who just got caught doing something they're not supposed to be doing.

I shrug. "Just the tail end." I pause, putting on a sunny disposition. "A spa weekend—that sounds phenomenal."

Catherine flicks her eyes to the floor as if trying to get out of punishment. "I don't have to go."

"What? That's ridiculous. Of course you have to go. A spa weekend sounds fantastic."

Catherine's eyes skate back up and land on my face. "You wouldn't be upset?"

"Why would I be upset?"

"Well, me leaving you when you have a hurt foot and all."

I have to choose my next words carefully if I want any shot at this freedom dangling over my head like a carrot.

"Catherine, please don't cancel your plans on account of me. It's only my foot. I can still take care of myself."

Catherine's forehead creases. *Great. She's unconvinced.* She studies me a bit harder. The blinds are drawn, and a draft travels across the back of my neck. It freaked me out when we first arrived, but Catherine was right. I am starting to get used to this old house.

"Are you absolutely sure?"

I must make it sound like I'll still miss her, that I'm not desperate to get her out of here so I can have the whole house to myself, without her hovering over me every time I sneeze or cough. If I act too eager, I'll hurt her feelings.

"I'm just going to be catching up on some work and rest. Nothing exciting. You won't miss a thing. Please, go have fun with your friends. Then come back feeling pampered and relaxed. I can't wait to hear all about it."

Catherine's eyes narrow. "Why are you wanting to get rid of me so badly?"

Shit. She's taking my reaction personally. My heart sinks like a heavy rock into my stomach. *Am I really being that transparent about my desperation to be alone?* She's not wrong, and somehow, she knows it.

"I'm not trying to get rid of you." I ignore the heat on my cheeks as I backpedal. "I would feel bad if you missed out on a fun trip just to stay with me. It's just a boot. It's annoying and a little inconvenient at times, sure, but it doesn't hinder me, like I said before. Unless you count walking with a limp." I smile. She doesn't.

"All right..." She still sounds doubtful. "If you really want to be alone, I can take a hint."

My stomach clenches. "Catherine, please don't take offense. It's not like that, really. I promise."

She breezes past me on her way upstairs. "I'll start packing, then. I know when I'm not welcome, even when it's in my own house."

Part of me wants to follow her up the stairs to beg and plead for forgiveness, but another part keeps me rooted where I stand. I take a few steadying breaths. I can get through whatever awkward hell this is.

But I can't figure out why she would rather spend her time and energy trying to make me feel guilty for encouraging her to go rather than looking forward to something that will bring her joy with her friends.

That night, I lie awake in bed, staring at the ceiling. I'm chasing sleep, but it's too far ahead of me, and I can't catch up.

The house is too quiet. There aren't even the usual groans and sighs from the walls and the plumbing. Eventually, my eyes start to burn, and sleep claims me, but it's fitful, severed by the unspoken tension between Catherine and me.

I wake early to the sound of banging around downstairs. After dressing, I head to the kitchen, where Catherine is slamming cabinet doors, buzzing around like a hornet.

"Everything all right?" I wrap my cardigan tighter around my chest. There's a chill in the air that has nothing to do with the temperature.

Catherine doesn't bat an eyelash, nor does she look at me when she says, "My taxi is picking me up in a few minutes. Enjoy your quality alone time that you want so much."

"Catherine, I didn't mean to hurt your feelings."

"My feelings aren't hurt." I can tell by her stiff posture and the wrinkle in her chin that she's lying, but I don't argue the point. "I'll see you when I get back."

I walk behind her to the door. She opens it and steps out onto the porch, acting as if she's not even going to turn around and say goodbye to me.

I delicately place a hand on her shoulder. "Have fun."

This gets her to turn around. Her eyes train on me. She nods and says, "Thanks," in a crisp voice before spinning back around and dragging her rolling suitcase with her. It makes a plunking noise on each step.

I watch her get into the taxi and pull out of the driveway, waving to her from the porch, but she doesn't dignify me with so much as a glance in my direction. Sighing, I go back inside and lock the door behind me. Then I hobble around the house, taking in the high ceilings and creaky floorboards. I haven't even been in so many rooms yet. Though I try to open a few closed doors, most of them are locked, which I find odd. I steer clear of her bedroom.

I look through a few kitchen drawers, more out of curiosity than anything. She has a junk drawer, much like every other human on the planet, filled with paper clips, batteries, rubber bands, and old bills. Then I make myself a coffee and walk out to the backyard. There's a nip in the air, and fog cloaks the grass. We've had a few sporadic days of sunshine, and now I crave the warmth on my skin. After draining the coffee, I head back inside to finish a project with a deadline and email it to the client when I'm finished.

At five o'clock on the dot, I order a pizza, wings, and a two-liter of soda. Catherine likes to stick to a restricted diet. There's nothing wrong with that or the organic meals she likes to prepare for us, but I am craving grease and cheese. Screw the diet for the weekend.

While I wait for the food to arrive, I make a playlist on my phone of my favorite songs and blast them through my Bluetooth speaker, something else I haven't been able to do since I got here. It's strange at first, listening to loud music in an old Victorian house where most of the furniture has existed since decades before I was even born.

The pizza arrives. I switch off the music and pull up my favorite binge-worthy shows on my laptop and start streaming while stuffing my face silly.

"I could get used to this," I say to no one. "Hope you can't see me right now, Catherine." I chuckle, glancing around the living room, wondering if she has hidden cameras planted in inconspicuous places. I wouldn't put it past her, although she's not very tech savvy.

Next, I saunter into the kitchen and look through the cabinets again, this time for any bottles of wine or maybe bourbon, wanting to pour myself a glass to relax and fall asleep with.

I'm standing in the pantry when the light goes off. An icy sensation sweeps across my skin, and goose bumps prickle on my arms, the hairs standing up. I immediately spin around, expecting to see someone standing there. *Did Catherine return? Is she playing a terrible joke on me?*

I squint through the darkness, trying to get my eyes to adjust. There's no one there. Still, I croak out a weak "Hello?" anyway.

I'm met by silence.

I flick the light switch, but it was still in the "up" position, so I toggle it a couple of times, and nothing happens. I step into the office, which is blanketed in shadows, and peek around the corner, licking my lips. The glow of my laptop is the only source of light there. Then I pad back to the living room and snatch my phone from the coffee table then tap the flashlight app on. My heart is pounding.

As I pan the light around the room, my breath squeezes out through my constricted throat. I strain my ears to hear movement, footsteps, anything.

I take a few steps around the room, trying to convince myself that the shadows crawling across the walls are being made from my phone's flashlight and nothing more.

Why would the power go out randomly? I glance at the basement door. It's shut and uninviting. I haven't been down there yet. Catherine didn't include that space in her initial tour of the house.

I don't like basements, even if I'm with someone else. They're creepy, claustrophobic, and usually freezing cold. Still, the breakers are probably down there. I haven't seen them anywhere else in the house. I walk toward the door, clamp my hand on the knob, and take a deep breath. *I can do this.* Then I swing the door open.

CHAPTER NINE

I'M STARING DOWN AT AN ABYSS OF DARKNESS, AFRAID TO EVEN PAN my flashlight into that depth. *What sinister nightmares might reveal themselves down there? Now, come on, Jess, monsters aren't real.* Neither is the ghost that Mark saw or the weird shadow upstairs. All the doors in the house are locked. Most of the windows are painted shut. This place is a fortress. No one can get in. The power only glitched. I just need to find the breakers and reset them. That's all.

Taking a deep breath, I plant my palm on the wall, which is made of gray cinder blocks. The concrete is cold, and there's no railing. Even at the top of the stairs, it already smells musty. Even the air is uninviting.

The wooden stairs are more like planks, half a century old, cracked in places and bowed out in others. With one hand, I hold my phone facing down, and the other hand stays flat against the wall. I start going down each step sideways, with my back against the opposite wall. The planks groan in protest, threatening to give out from under me. I try not to think about plummeting through and breaking my other ankle. I focus on one step at a time, trying not to put too much weight on the boot.

When I finally reach the bottom, I breathe a sigh of relief that one, I made it without falling, and two, none of the shadows are moving. Still, I can't shake the feeling that I'm being watched. It's a prickly sensation in the pit of my stomach.

Goose bumps travel across my skin because of the cold as I pan the phone around. The basement ceiling is low, barely six feet. A tall person would have to bend at certain angles to stand up straight. It's a closed-in space, and the mountains of boxes against each wall make it even more claustrophobic.

After spotting the breaker box on the wall in the corner, I limp toward it, having to weave around a row of boxes and trunks. Catherine seems like a pack rat. Maybe she's one of those nostalgic types who doesn't like to throw things away. I wonder whether the main sections of her house would be more cluttered if she didn't have the attic and basement spaces to utilize.

Opening the breaker box, I hold up the flashlight. I'm thankful they're all labeled and in good condition other than a few cobwebs I have to swat away.

I flick the switch labeled Basement. At first, there's a clicking sound, then a faint buzzing, and finally, the lights come on. With a sigh of relief, I hit the ones that say First Floor and Second Floor next, then Third Floor.

Then I trudge back to the stairs, my eyes grazing over boxes of what look like Catherine's old clothes, and peer up. The lights are on upstairs. Relief floods me, and my shoulders relax.

I'm getting ready to head back upstairs, to put as much space between me and this basement as possible, when something catches my eye. It's another photo album, half-hidden under a boho dress of sheer flower-print fabric. I lift the dress and pick up the album. It captures my attention because on the front is a little plastic cover with Catherine's handwriting. *Mark—baby.* Something else I find interesting about it is the fact that it's not dusty like the rest of the albums and books near it. It looks recently touched. It's on top of everything else, as if the person who put it there wanted easy access to it, and the placement at the bottom of the stairs is also a bit curious.

I open it and start looking through it, laughing at a picture of Mark wearing a cowboy costume at what looks like a Halloween party. He has a serious expression on his face, and his hand is on his hip, touching the holster of his plastic toy gun. He looks adorable in the boots and hat. I take a quick snap of the picture with my phone so I can send it to him later.

After perusing the rest of the album, I close it to put it back exactly where I found it on top of the box, but something falls out of the slit at the bottom.

I reach to pick it up. A Ziploc bag with several envelopes inside. Curiosity gets the better of me, and I remove the first one. I know I shouldn't be doing this, but I can't help myself. Gently, I pull the letter out of the open envelope.

Then I gasp.

I can't believe what I'm reading. I read the letter twice, first skimming the neat cursive, then again, more carefully. My heart hammers against my chest. The letter burns my fingertips as if it's going to come alive and ignite a spark in my face. This can't be real. It can't be right. *What the hell is going on in this house?* After reading the letter, I have more questions than answers. My brain whirls at a million miles an hour as I desperately try to figure out what all this means.

The one thing I am sure of is Catherine Hawley is a liar.

CHAPTER TEN

THE LETTER IS UNDATED, BUT THE PAPER IT'S WRITTEN ON IS TINGED yellow with age. I read it through so many times I start to memorize it. It's addressed to Catherine, from a woman named Lily.

Catherine, it begins, and I notice how it's very formal, no *Dear* attached to it. I try to piece together any clues that will give this letter more meaning.

> Freddy passed away. As you might assume, I'm devastated. I never asked for any of this, of course. You destroyed everything. How can you sleep at night? How does the guilt not eat you alive, Catherine?
>
> I'm probably a fool to even assume you'll read this letter. You'll probably throw it away as soon as you find out it's from me, but I don't care. I'm going to send it anyway. Say what I need to say. You might argue and claim I'm projecting, but I have to

get these feelings out into the universe. I can't bottle them up inside anymore. They're detrimental to my mental health or what's left of it. Again, something you destroyed. I want you to take responsibility, Catherine. There need to be consequences to your actions.

I want to see Mark. You owe me that much. If you don't agree to let me see him, I might have to take matters into my own hands.

I'll admit you had me fooled at first. In the beginning, I thought I might be wrong, but it's too hard to deny it now. Mark looks exactly like my husband. I know he's my real son, and Freddy was really yours. I was so stupid back then. I didn't read between the lines, or maybe I couldn't. There's testing for this kind of thing, you know, to prove it. I know what you've done.

Even my husband seems to think I've gone off the deep end. He's resorted to calling me crazy, but I don't care if he doesn't believe me. I know Mark is my real son. Call it mother's intuition.

Do the right thing, Catherine. Don't take him away from me again. Let me see him. Don't make me get attorneys involved in this. Trust me. You don't want to go down that road.

I'll be waiting to hear back. If you know what's good for you, you'll have opened this letter and read every word, and now the crippling guilt is eating you alive.

Let me in, Catherine. I deserve this slice of human decency after what you've done to me, after the hell you've put me through. Freddy is gone. At least give me peace by letting me spend time with Mark.

—Lily

CHAPTER ELEVEN

I STAND THERE WITH THE LETTER IN MY HAND, THE PAPER SCORCHING my fingertips as if it's on fire. I stare down at the words until they blur into patches of ink. If what this Lily woman is claiming is true, then Catherine switched another baby in the hospital for Mark and got away with it.

The letters are not recent, at least not from what I can tell. My brain can't rationalize Mark being abducted as a child, but if it's true, then Catherine obviously saw no consequences. *What has happened in between? Did she eventually placate this woman by letting her have the access to Mark she requested?* A million questions cut through my mind like a buzz saw, ripping my peaceful solitude to shreds.

I take the entire bundle of letters upstairs with me, spread them out on the coffee table in the living room, and stare down at them.

I shouldn't have opened the first letter, shouldn't have snooped into something that isn't my business, but this isn't about my crossing invisible boundaries anymore. This is about my husband and the potential that his entire life has been a lie.

The concept of Catherine lying to him, tricking him, making him believe she was his real mother, makes my stomach hurt. I hug my arms around my chest.

Most of the letters are about Lily begging Catherine to let her see Mark, more threats of lawyer involvement if Catherine doesn't follow through. I pull out one of the letters tucked behind the others at the bottom. This one is not in Lily's handwriting. It's in Catherine's. It has an address, the words scribbled as if she had to write it in a hurry. I take a picture of it then look it up online. The address matches with Cedar Pointe Hospital, thirty minutes from Catherine's house.

The letters from Lily are filled with rants but nothing that mentions why her son, or Catherine's real son, died or what age he was at the time of his death. I assume he was young, but it must have been at least several years after he was born if not longer, because in some of the letters, she talks about how she and Catherine got the boys together for playdates and Lily missed that.

None of it makes any sense.

What was Catherine's motive for all this? Was her husband involved?

If Mark had any idea or even a suspicion, he would have told me, or he would have been trying to find his true birth mother now that he's an adult. He's never mentioned anyone by the name of Lily or Freddy before.

I read another letter. This one is short and to the point, but the maliciousness is there. You can hear the frost in this scorned woman's voice through her writing.

Steven and I are fighting a lot lately. I blame you, Catherine. I just want you to know that. Thanks

> *to you, I have nothing. There is a wedge between me and Steven now, and my son—well, your son—is dead. You must have known deep down this was going to happen. You knew Freddy would get sick. That's why you did this. You found an easy target, but I'm here to let you know one thing, you cold and calculating bitch. You won't get away with this. I won't lie down and be the victim anymore.*
>
> *You took my son. You robbed me of my own flesh and blood, of years, a lifetime with my real child. You destroyed my family. You took what belonged to me. You are a thief, Catherine. You can't just switch babies in a hospital and expect to get away with it.*

I take a picture of this letter along with a few others and move them from my main camera reel to store them in a separate, private folder on my phone just in case.

A shudder jogs up my spine. I fold the letter back and drop it on the table, as I can't look at it anymore. It's making me sick. I need more proof. This woman could be suffering from a mental illness or postpartum depression that never healed. She's blaming Catherine for all her problems, for the death of her son, for swapping out babies.

If it's true, then why would Catherine save all these letters? Why not just burn them and get rid of the evidence? They were stacked next to photo albums that anyone could find, eventually including Mark if he got curious enough.

Is it possible that Catherine forgot about them over the years? Or were they meticulously placed there? Why not try to hide them once she knew Mark and I would be moving in? And what happened to Lily? Where is she now? Why did the letters stop? Obviously, there were never any charges pressed. If so, Mark wouldn't still be with Catherine, if it had been proved he wasn't really her son.

There are still too many chunks of missing information that I can't work out. It's giving me a headache. I take a deep breath and shove all the letters back into the Ziploc bag precisely in the order they were in before. Then I trudge back down the creaky stairs and put them back in the basement, placing them exactly where I found them. By the time I reach the top of the stairs again, I'm sweating, and my injured leg is aching.

I limp around the living room and kitchen, going through the motions of cleaning up and getting ready for bed the way I would on any normal night, but this is anything but a normal night. My head is spinning with distraction, and I can't concentrate on any of my tasks.

The glass I used earlier slips from my hand as I reach to put it back in the cabinet after I wash it. It shatters into a million pieces over the counter and floor.

I curse under my breath and start picking up the shards from the counter. A piece of jagged glass knicks my thumb, and I suck in a deep breath, watching the blood pool at the pad. I run it under the faucet and press a paper towel to it until I can get a bandage from upstairs. I sweep up the remaining pieces with a broom, brushing over the area several times to make sure I get it all.

Then I switch off the lights downstairs and start climbing to my bedroom on the floor above. By now, I despise all stairs. Maybe Mark and I should buy a one-level home once we're able.

I stop at the landing. Something doesn't feel right. It's like the house is unsettled and feeding off my nervous energy.

Glancing over my shoulder, I hobble down the hallway, the floorboards groaning under my feet. I keep the lights on in the hall, and when I get to my room, I debate sleeping with my bedroom lights on too.

I wash my face, but I can't recognize the woman blinking back at me in the mirror. *How am I supposed to keep this information to myself? Will Catherine notice if I'm acting strange around her?* It's like worms are wriggling underneath my skin.

Do I call Mark immediately, tonight, and tell him what I've discovered? Or do I sit on it, bide my time, and try to dig up more about it before I get him involved?

He's overseas, already under tremendous pressure to make partner at his advertising firm. He doesn't need more stress added to his life. Besides, I don't know the full story of this drama. For now, all I have to go on are the ramblings of a woman that sound like psychotic breaks.

I climb into bed and pull the covers up to my chin even though it's torturously hot in this room. Normally, it's so drafty in the house, and I'm always cold, but not tonight. Tonight, my body is a furnace, burning from within, bursting at the seams with this new development.

I'm tortured with indecision. Tell Mark. Don't tell Mark. The words clatter around in my head alongside the thump of my heart. The wind whistles against the windowpane, almost as if weeping for me. The house feels too enormous right now, like it's going to fold in on itself and swallow me with it.

Every sound sets me off. Every time I am near drifting, another noise snaps me back to consciousness. Catherine will be home tomorrow. I'll have to make my decision to either confront this or bottle it up before then.

CHAPTER TWELVE

You took my son. You robbed me of my own flesh and blood, of years, a lifetime with my real child. You destroyed my family. You took what belonged to me. You are a thief, Catherine. You can't just switch babies in a hospital and expect to get away with it.

The words from the letter sting my eyes, like I'm staring directly into the sun, burning my corneas.

I can't get those words out of my head. They're like lashes from a whip. The wounds are embedded now, taking root, spreading paranoia within me. I'm pacing in the living room, stopping every few seconds to look out the window, waiting for Catherine's arrival.

I've hobbled around on my boot to tidy the house, putting everything back where it belongs, taking out the trash, and making the kitchen and living room spotless. I even lit a few candles, but then I blew them out, not wanting to seem overly eager.

THE MOTHER-IN-LAW

Even though I felt pathetic the whole time I was doing it, I've been practicing my greeting to her in the mirror. I don't want to come off as stiff or overly friendly or guarded or too enthusiastic. I need to be somewhere in the middle of all that—reserved. After all, things were still slightly strained between us when she left.

Now I don't know how to behave around her once she returns. I wring my hands together, take my hundredth sip of water, and run my hands through my hair. Then I stare out the window again.

There's nothing going on out there. You can't even see the main road from the house. It's so isolated, sitting on a huge plot of land, acres and acres of nothing.

Maybe this Lily person didn't know how to find Catherine. Perhaps Catherine controlled their meeting places and kept the rest of her life cryptic. It certainly wouldn't be hard to do. A person could hide away here without being found.

Shuddering, I gulp. I don't want to think about the logistics of that or the fact that my husband is a million miles away and can't help me.

I am sitting on this landmine of information, ready to explode from within, like confetti littering the room.

Part of me doesn't want to believe any of it, that Catherine could even be capable of stealing someone else's baby and swapping it with her own. *Why wouldn't she want her own child, the one she gave birth to? Did she somehow know her baby was sick?* All I can think is that Catherine or her husband or both of them knew about a genetic issue and went to extreme lengths to make sure they had a healthy child.

Mark is that child. And boy, did he certainly grow up to be a healthy man. I've barely seen Mark get a cold. If what Lily says is right, they robbed her of bringing up a healthy, handsome boy like my husband.

The thought makes me nauseous.

Maybe this Lily woman is just crazy, off her meds, or grief-stricken from her son's death, and the devastation pulled her under like a rip current. I have a lot of unanswered questions to address. *For one thing—how does Lily know Catherine's home address? How are these two women linked, aside from the baby-swapping issue?*

When I look out the window again, I see Catherine's taxi crawling up the drive, the gravel pluming around the tires. My palms are sweating, and my pulse hammers through my eardrums. Blood rushes to my head, warming my face and making me dizzy. I remind myself that if I panic, she'll know something's off.

She gets out of the car and walks around to the trunk to lift out her suitcase. Then she pulls out a large gift bag. It's teal, with silver polka dots and silver tissue paper bursting from the top.

Impulsively, I open the door to greet her. "Hi, Catherine." My voice sounds rusty. I clear my throat and plant on a welcoming smile.

Her eyes light up when she sees me, as if all the weirdness between us has been forgotten on her end. Maybe it has. Perhaps a relaxing spa weekend was the cure she needed. I'm suddenly envious of all the pampering she must have received. I need to find a way to relax for myself. But I'm pretty sure that ship sailed after I found the letters.

"It's good to see you. How was your weekend?" My voice is way too high and squeaky.

"It was lovely." Catherine breathes out a luxurious sigh, and her eyelashes flutter. Her silver hair is pulled back in an impeccable bun. A string of pearls decorates her neck. She's wearing white cotton pants that mold to her trim legs and a cream-colored cardigan, the buttons the color of oyster pearls, buttoned all the way to the slender curve of her collar bone.

"Let me help you," I offer, reaching for her suitcase even though I'm balancing on my boot.

She hands me the gift bag instead. "For you."

"That's very kind," I say. "Thank you so much."

We get inside, the only sound between us the rolling of her suitcase across the floor. She stops in the living room and looks around. My breathing stills until she speaks.

"It's good to be home."

"I'll bet."

I'm standing in the doorway, awkwardly holding the gift bag.

Catherine's eyes graze over it. "Don't you want to open your present?"

I snap out of my stupor. "Right! Of course. You really shouldn't have, Catherine."

"I wanted to do something nice for you." Catherine's smile brightens the caramel flecks in her eyes.

"That's so kind." I nod, take the bag to the couch, and start peeling back the layers of tissue paper on the top.

I pull the items out one at a time—a loofah, a set of foot creams, face masks, hair serum, a wooden massage roller that fits in my palm, a neck pillow, and a set of washcloths that are so soft it's like touching a cloud.

"Catherine, this is a wonderful set of gifts. Thank you so much."

"I take care of the people I love." A twinkle gleams in her eyes.

Carefully, I put everything back in the bag. "I'll be sure to use all these things. In fact, I'll take them upstairs now and put them in my bathroom so you can get settled. We can have something easy for dinner. Soup and sandwiches or something."

Catherine's smile remains plastered to her face. "That sounds like a perfect evening."

It's far from perfect, but given the circumstances, it's all I can do to keep from squirming in front of her. Part of me is telling me to run, but I have nowhere else to go.

Japan, maybe. But even a ticket would clear out my savings. *Then what? Just show up at his office and announce that his parents stole him from a hospital?* Plus, there's the logistics. I'm okay pottering around the house, but travelling anywhere far in this foot brace would be a struggle. Besides, even if Catherine did do something bad thirty years ago, it doesn't mean she's going to harm me. I'm her daughter-in-law. If anything, her only crime since I arrived is being *too* nice.

Yes, too nice,'to the point that it's kinda pathological. Shit. I'm stuck here until he returns, and I'm going to have to figure out how to live with this woman in this dark and cold house when I fear that deep down, she might be quietly unhinged and harboring a dark secret.

CHAPTER THIRTEEN

I WAKE UP JUST AS THE SILVER OF DAWN BECOMES A HAZY LAVENDER. While Catherine is still asleep, I get out of bed and fill the bathtub to the top. I miss showers. Having to hang my leg out the side of the bath every day is starting to become a chore. I wash up quickly, hoping for clarity and success today in what I need to accomplish.

Afterward, I make my bed but sit on it, propping myself against the headboard with my pillows behind me. My laptop is open, and I'm in an aggressive focus zone, but it has nothing to do with work.

I type in the name *Lily* into the search bar and beside it, *Cedar Pointe*, the closest town to where we are. Then I scroll through the options. Nothing looks right. Frustrated, I try a different tactic. I type in *Lily and Freddy* but also get nothing. Then I type in different variations of spellings of the names, inserting *Mark* and *Catherine* in there, too, and using their last names. I don't have Lily's last name, unfortunately, so I hit a brick wall in my sleuthing.

I'm so focused that when there's a knock at my bedroom door, it makes me jump a mile.

"Come in," I say, frantically trying to close all my open tabs about trying to dig up dirt on this elusive Lily.

Catherine springs into the room, all grace, shoulders straight and poised, a smile on her painted-red lips. She's carrying a tray. On the tray is a small white clear-glass vase with a single pink carnation poking out the top. There's a plate of eggs, bacon, and toast with jam in the center. Another glass, this one filled to the brim with orange juice, rests beside the plate of food.

I sit up straight, thankful that I decided to get up early. For once, I'm ready for one of Catherine's little impromptu visits to my room.

"Good morning," she chirps and sets the tray down on the bed beside me.

"What's this for?" I stare at the plate then her.

"Can't your mother-in-law bring you breakfast in bed?" She blinks, the picture of innocence.

"Sure..."

"The eggs came from a farm down the road. They are as fresh as it gets."

"I'm sure they're delicious."

"Go on and have a bite," she urges, her eyes trained on me.

I pick up the fork, give her as polite a smile as I can muster, and stab the fork prongs into a fluffy piece of egg. It's so buttery and smooth I almost moan with delight. It's delicious. So good that I'm willing to forgive Catherine for forgetting I don't usually eat breakfast.

"Well?" Catherine's eyebrows perk.

"Incredible," I say while chewing, then I take another bite. I can't resist. It's just too good.

Catherine raises her arm and brushes her fingers softly against the hair next to my cheek. It's so sudden and unexpected that I instinctively flinch. Catherine chuckles, her laughter like a windchime tinkling against a soft breeze.

"What's wrong, dear?" she asks.

"Nothing."

"Are you frightened of me or something?" Her grin is like a tight rubber band, ready to snap.

"Of course not." I shake my head, trying to be convincing, but I can't tell if she's buying it.

Catherine glances at my laptop. "Working in bed this morning?"

"Just catching up on some emails," I lie.

"You should stay in bed while you work today," Catherine suggests. "Rest your ankle as much as you can so it will heal faster. I can bring you all your meals."

"Actually, I was thinking about going out today," I say on the fly,

"Going out?" Catherine's laughter is like an abrupt bang ricocheting across the walls. "Where would you go? And how? With that foot?" She points at my boot and frowns.

I wish she wouldn't treat it like a disability. I don't understand why she's in here, fussing over me and bringing me breakfast in bed. Her doting isn't sincere. It's suspicious, especially after how we left off before she went away for the weekend.

"I just need to get out of the house for a little while." I keep my tone as casual as possible. "You know, fresh air and whatnot."

"You can walk around the grounds and get all the fresh air you like," Catherine counters with a slight edge.

"I know." I shrug. "I thought about going to the library and maybe find a few books to check out and read on lazy days around the house."

"I'll go with you."

"That's not necessary, Catherine." I shovel more eggs into my mouth and don't look at her.

"At least let me organize a taxi for you." She's defensive now and not trying to cover it up behind superficial laughter.

"You don't have to do all these things for me, Catherine. I'm perfectly capable." I soften the blow by giving her a tender smile. "Although I do appreciate it. I don't want to become a burden for you. I'm already a guest in your house. You're doing enough. Trust me."

"You aren't a burden to me," Catherine insists, a flame in her eyes now. "And you're like a daughter to me. Hardly a guest."

I don't know what to say to that, so I chew on my bottom lip and stare down at my plate of half-eaten food.

An awkward silence hangs in the space between us. My pulse flutters. Coals burn in my cheeks. You could slice through the layer of tension with a knife.

"If you want to go out by yourself, you're certainly allowed to, although I don't recommend it." She pauses then adds in a darker tone, "You're not a prisoner here."

"It's nothing against you. I just want to get away for a little while. I won't be gone that long."

Catherine stands up and rubs her palms against the pleats in her red leggings. "Do what you want. Enjoy the rest of your breakfast. I'll be back to check on you soon."

I have no idea what constitutes "soon," but I probably need to get out of here before "soon" occurs again.

* * *

I wait around, timing my escape for when I know she'll be in the shower after tending to her garden for a good portion of the morning. Just before lunch, I send her a quick text to let her know I'm headed out—avoiding as much confrontation with her as possible—then my Uber driver picks me up at the end of Catherine's long driveway.

The driver talks on the phone through an earpiece the entire ride, saving me from having to make conversation with a stranger, before dropping me off in front of the library. It's bigger than I expected, with a wide set of concrete steps leading up to a huge arched awning. The steps are a little intimidating, but I'm capable of limping up with the help of the handrail.

The minute I step inside, I'm hit with a wave of nostalgia from the scent of old books, the crinkly sounds of a page turning, the whispers, and the clacking of fingertips against computer keyboards. Under normal circumstances, I would be at peace and would want to spend hours here, just browsing and reading through books and magazines to my heart's content. But I'm on a mission. I need to find out who Lily really is.

From a librarian at the reception desk, I get a code to be able to use one of the computers in the archives room. I looked it up ahead of time—they have a section available to search through genealogy records. I don't know if it's because it's a small town or that's just something I can get easy access to, but I'll pay a fee to obtain birth records if I can find them.

It's quiet in this section of the library, and I'm thankful I'm alone. My heart batters like bird wings against my ribcage. I'm not sure if I even want to know the answers to my questions. But I do know that I can't face talking to Mark until I have some concrete evidence to help me. There's no way I can call him and tell him about the letters. Knowing Mark and how close he is with Catherine, I'm sure all he'll do is ask his mom. Then Catherine will lie. She'll convince Mark that Lily is crazy. Honestly, Lily might be, but I'm not taking Catherine's word for it.

Through trial and error, I finally find Lily. It's a common name, and I have to comb through several dozen lists, but I am able to link her to the specific area around Cedar Pointe. Her name is Lily Roberts, and I'm able to fit the missing puzzle piece in by confirming that she married Steven Roberts, whom she'd referred to in a few of her letters. His name is spelled the same way. She's also around the same age as Catherine. It has to be her. This is the biggest clue I've been able to find so far.

I sit back in my chair, dazed and staring at the screen, astounded by what I've been able to find. I'm one step closer to discovering the next link in this ominous story.

CHAPTER FOURTEEN

The house smells like lemon when I walk in the front door. Catherine is waiting in the foyer, and I wonder how long she's been standing there to greet me.

"How was the library?" she asks, stretching her smile.

I try not to cringe away from her sickly-sweet expression. "It was good."

"What did you pick out?" Catherine glances at the bag on my shoulder. I knew better than to come home empty-handed.

"A few romance novels." I let out a nervous laugh. "Something to occupy me while Mark is away." Then I wince because that came out wrong.

Catherine doesn't seem to notice, though. "Follow me." She beckons me with a bony wrist. "I made a lemon cake with a lemon curd filling and a cream cheese icing."

"That's what that heavenly smell is?"

"Yes." Catherine beams.

She leads me into the kitchen, where a glimmer of natural light filters in through the bay window. The sky is overcast, and there's a soft breeze. Leaves wave on the branches, and a crow caws on one of the limbs as the clouds roll past.

The cake is sitting in the center of the island. Catherine already has plates and forks out beside it along with two napkins and tea already steeped and poured into mugs.

"Wow. You got all this ready for me? But I didn't tell you when I'd be back."

Catherine makes a clean slice with the knife through the cake. "Never doubt a mother's intuition." Her grin splits wide open, and she slides a cake piece onto my plate. "Eat up, dear. There's plenty."

"I'm going to gain a hundred pounds by the time I move out," I joke.

"Nonsense." Catherine laughs delicately. She puts a piece for herself on the additional plate.

When I take the first bite, the flavors burst in my mouth. The sponge is moist and the filling creamy. I haven't eaten such a perfect cake for years, if ever.

"Well?" Catherine gazes at me, expectant.

"It's as delicious as it looks," I admit.

Catherine's shoulders straighten with pride. "I've been working on it since you left." Her smile fades suddenly. "I wish you'd waited until I got out of the shower so I could've at least said goodbye this morning."

An uncomfortable sensation crawls across my spine. "Well, I'm here now," I force out and take a sip of the lemon-and-honey tea.

I devour the last bite and rise to take the empty plate to the sink to wash it, but Catherine clamps her hand on my arm, stopping me.

"I'll take care of the dishes, darling."

"Are you sure?"

"Of course."

"Well, if you don't mind, I'm going upstairs to freshen up and put my books away. I need to finish up some tasks for work too."

"Disappearing again so soon?"

She's trying to make me feel guilty, but I won't take the bait.

"Just for a little while. I have clients who need me."

"Well, you know where to find me if *you* need *me*," she emphasizes.

"Thanks."

I head upstairs and close my door with a gentle click then sit on my bed and make a video call to Mark while I open my laptop, propping it on my thighs.

"Hey, baby." Seeing his face immediately floods me with a sense of calmness.

Mark's sitting in bed, too, wearing no shirt, his broad shoulders and washboard abs exposed. He looks thinner, a little paler, but there's still a vibrancy in his face, a glow in his cheeks. His dark hair is mussed, as if he's been lying on the pillows. A bedside lamp is on beside him, and I see a book propped open in his lap. I want to be there touching his warm skin, kissing his soft lips, and feeling the rhythm of his heartbeat against my palm and the rush of his breathing against the back of my neck as we spoon while we fall asleep.

I'm so desperate for this type of intimacy in that moment that my eyes fill with tears. His eyes are the color of clouds, and the depth inside them creates a nuclear reaction in me. The tears spill over my cheeks.

"What's wrong?" He sits up straight.

"It's nothing." I swipe my hand through the air. "I'm just having a hard time right now. I miss you so much."

"I miss you, too, baby, so much." Mark gives me a sympathetic smile, but there is also a hint of pity that makes me plunge into a deeper despair.

"Tell me what's going on there."

I debate telling him what I discovered in the basement and the borderline-obsessive investigating I've been doing ever since.

Instead, I start venting. "Your mom is being too nice to me."

He bursts out laughing. "What?"

"I know it sounds ridiculous." I glance at the door, and my eyes steer to the crack underneath it to make sure I don't see a shadow of her feet there. I've learned to expect anything at this point, so I wouldn't be surprised if she were standing there with her ear pressed to the door.

I keep my voice down anyway. "You don't understand. She won't leave me alone. She makes me breakfast in bed. I just came home from the library, and she had this homemade lemon cake that looks like it came off the front cover of a baking magazine. Tea steeped just the way I like it and everything."

Mark quirks an eyebrow. "Honey, am I missing something? That all sounds fantastic. I wish someone were here waiting on me hand and foot."

I roll my eyes. "Don't hold your breath."

Mark gives an easy laugh. I wish I could feel that way right now, but instead, unease spreads through my body like a virus.

"I think you're reading too much into it."

"Easy for you to say. You're not here."

"You're being bratty. I love it when you're bratty." He grins—devilish, handsome, irresistible. His bedroom eyes undress me. It's night where he is.

My pulse spikes with desire, but instead, I say, "You aren't taking my feelings seriously."

He rolls his eyes. "Okay, well, what is it that's *really* bothering you, then?"

"I just like my personal space, you know? I don't like being doted over. I can't breathe. I mean, it's nice and all. It's just a little... too much."

"Overbearing?"

"Yes, and something else. Too enthusiastic. To the point that it doesn't seem genuine."

"I know you like your alone time, but try not to take it personally. You have to remember she's been alone in that house for a long time. She's practically giddy to have company for once, someone she can spoil."

"I'm just not used to it. That's all."

"Why not enjoy it while it lasts?"

"I guess..." I'm frustrated that Mark doesn't seem to comprehend the full scale of Catherine's excessive doting. It's like she's trying too hard, but I can't figure out the "why" part yet. It seems to be getting worse too.

"Anyway," I say, not wanting to talk about it anymore because I'm hitting a brick wall with him and I need a change in topic. "How are things in Tokyo?"

"The food is amazing."

"For a foodie like you, I can only imagine."

"I'm learning a few phrases too." He chuckles. "Mostly curse words, though."

"Ha! Why doesn't that surprise me?"

"You know me." He shrugs, looking boyish.

"Everything with work is going well too?"

"Yep." He yawns and stretches. "Right on pace with everything."

"Partner looking good?"

"Within reach."

"That's great, baby. I'm so proud of you. And happy too," I say with a grin, meaning every word.

He gets a frisky gleam in his eye. "Can I have a bedtime treat before I fall asleep?"

I give him a smirk. "How did I know that was coming?"

"Come on, baby," he whines. "I need a release, and your beautiful face is right here. I know you need it too. You look tired and stressed out."

"You sure know how to charm a woman."

"Oh, come on, Jess. You know I'm just teasing."

"All right." I laugh, knowing I won't be able to resist his request for a FaceTime phone-sex session. It won't be the same as the real thing, but it's better than nothing. "Let me just lock my door first."

I put on my headphones, connect them to the Bluetooth of my phone, and quietly submerge myself into a digital form of intimacy with my husband. The sweet release is everything I need right now.

* * *

Comforted and relaxed, I settle in to work, this time at the desk in the office so Catherine won't get the impression I'm holed up in my room on purpose just to avoid her.

But I don't do my normal work. I'm going to get behind on my projects, but I can't seem to steer myself away from Lily.

I type her name into the search bar, but I get nothing, so I type her name then *Cedar Pointe*. Still nothing. I type in *Freddy Roberts, death*. I get a few hits, but none of them is the same Freddy. The other five deceased Freddy Robertses I was able to find all died in the age range of fifty to eighty.

The sun pokes out from behind a cloud, sending a stream of canary-yellow light filtering across my desk. I stare at the tiny dust orbs swirling in the sunbeam then try another series of search phrases. Steven Roberts's name pops up for an address on the other side of town.

Next, I enter the address into Maps and find out it's located about twenty-five minutes away. He also has an old LinkedIn profile showing he's a retired pharmaceutical rep. I type his address into my phone and start mentally preparing to go visit him.

What harm can it do to try? The worst that can happen is he slams the door in my face or it's the wrong Steven Roberts. But the Steven Roberts on LinkedIn is the only one listed for this area. It has to be him. I just have to be optimistic that he'll be willing to talk to me. I'll take my handheld bottle of mace that I take on runs sometimes in case things go south.

Satisfied that I've made some progress, I limp down the hallway, the house's draft cooling my skin, the lanterns glowing, fake flames dancing, casting shadows on the walls. The floors creak under my feet.

I turn the corner and immediately collide with Catherine.

She's carrying a laundry hamper with clothes—*my clothes*—neatly folded inside it.

I gawk, staring from the clothes to her then back again. "What's all this?"

"I took the liberty of doing your washing for you," Catherine boasts.

"You—washed my clothes? Where did you find them?"

"In the dirty clothes hamper in your room, silly."

"You went into my room and got my dirty clothes from my hamper?"

The blood drains from my face. All I can think about is my

dirty underwear that she would have seen... touched... and God knows what else.

"I used to do Mark's laundry all the time when he came to visit. He didn't seem to mind." Catherine gives me that innocent smile I've come to know all too well.

"Well, as nice a gesture as I'm sure you thought it was, I would rather just wash my own clothes next time. For privacy reasons."

Catherine rolls her eyes and swats her hand playfully against my arm. "You are always so worried about privacy, darling. There's nothing to hide. We're both adult women here." She eyes me up and down. "What are you doing on this side of the house?"

"I was just on my way to the kitchen to get a glass of water."

She pats my arm. "I'll take your laundry upstairs and put it on your bed for you."

"I can handle putting it away. Thanks."

She says nothing more as she struts off down the hallway with the laundry basket bouncing off her hip, disappearing around a corner to take it up the stairs to my room.

I'm rooted in place, temporarily forgetting my thirst, watching her go and wondering what boundaries she'll cross next and whether I'll be able to handle it.

Then a thought occurs to me. Even though I closed the tabs on my laptop from my search, I left the address on my phone, which was still in the office unsupervised. What if Catherine wants to snoop on my phone? I have no evidence that she would, but she was in my room. What if doing the laundry is a cover for her poking through my things? I can't risk her sneaking back down the stairs while I'm elsewhere in the house. I hurry down the hall, practically dragging the boot. A nervous sweat covers my skin as a deep-rooted fear blossoms inside me. I try to draw in a deep breath, but my throat is constricting. The house goes silent, listening and watching me, feeding off my paranoia, eager.

I pop my head into the office, bracing myself, preparing to come up with excuses, but it's empty. I clutch my hand to my heart when I realize my phone is there, undisturbed, the screen black and locked. Catherine is nowhere in sight, and it doesn't look like she's been through here at all. I breathe a sigh of relief. There may be nothing to hide around here, but at least my snooping will be kept secret for now. I need to keep my investigation buried for as long as possible.

CHAPTER FIFTEEN

When I wake the next morning, the house is quiet. I walk down the stairs. Moving with the boot is second nature now. The first thing I notice that's out of the ordinary is that Catherine is not zipping around everywhere, full of energy, following me around, asking me what I need.

This is a first. I head to the kitchen and start a pot of fresh coffee, since it doesn't look like Catherine has done that yet. I glance at the clock on the microwave, frowning. It's after nine. She should definitely be up by now. Usually, she would have completed a hundred tasks already.

I walk to the fridge to grab the milk and find a note attached to it with a magnet of the Statue of Liberty.

In Catherine's whimsical cursive is:

Jess, I had to head into town to run a few errands. You were sleeping so soundly this morning and looked so peaceful I didn't want to wake you. I'll be back soon. In the meantime, get some rest and

work done, and we can catch up later in the afternoon.
  Toodles!
  —Catherine

I read the note again, my cheeks flushed with irritation. This reaches a whole new level of invasiveness. *Did she really just admit to coming into my room and watching me sleep? Did she snoop through my things?* Thank goodness my phone has a lock on it. Maybe I should start locking my door before I go to bed every night. Then again, I wouldn't put it past Catherine to find a way in or get super offended if she noticed.

Fueled by my frustration, I get dressed, call another Uber, then wait at the end of the driveway to be picked up. I'm not even thinking, just making blind, potentially irrational decisions. They might come back to haunt me, but I can't be in that house another second where I feel like I'm constantly being watched.

The house feels alive somehow. Maybe I'm just paranoid, reading too much into this. Either way, I need to get out of here for a little while. It will be easier to do that while Catherine is gone.

This is going to be an unannounced, potentially unwelcome visit. Steven Roberts might not even be home. But I have to try. He's retired, so I'm hoping my odds are better. That, and it's Saturday morning. Most people are home on Saturday mornings. It's a safe bet.

I greet the Uber driver. This time, it's an elderly man with bony wrists and thinning hair the color of the moon pulled back into a low ponytail. He's wearing a shirt with a picture of a wolf on it. He tries to make banal conversation with me, but

I keep my answers short and one worded, staring at my phone. Eventually, he gives up and turns up the radio.

I know Mark is probably going to start questioning all these ride charges. The Uber account is linked to our bank, so if he's checking it, he's going to see that I'm taking Ubers all over town. I need to think of an excuse to give him, but for now, my head is swimming through all the scenarios of how this meeting with Steven Roberts might go.

The Uber driver pulls up in front of the house.

"This is it. Have a great day!"

"Thanks."

I open the door then stand there for a beat after he drives away.

Then I glance down at the app to make sure there are other drivers in the vicinity if I need to leave quickly.

The house is tucked away on a quiet cul-de-sac. It's small but charming, a bungalow-type cottage made of red brick and black shutters with a matching paneled door. The roof slopes at the top, and there's a fireplace on the side. Two portrait windows are on either side of the door. Blue hydrangeas are in full bloom, and the lawn is green. The house is cozy with warm curb appeal, the opposite of Catherine's gothic estate. Even the air feels warmer here.

I take a deep breath and wipe my palms on my jeans then take a few steps toward the house. A ringing in my ears and lightheadedness makes me feel like my head isn't attached to my body but floating just above it. My legs are so heavy with doubt that it's like I'm clomping through mud.

Climbing the two steps to the front door, I see that they have a doorbell camera. I press the button, watching the little circle in the center light up blue, and wait. A few seconds later, footsteps sound from inside. My breath catches in my throat as the door swings open, and a man stands there, curiously peering at me. He's tall, with gray stubble, dark hair on his arms, and he's wearing a white T-shirt and black joggers. He looks athletic, in his early sixties if I had to guess.

His eyes trail down to my boot. "Can I help you?"

"Are you Steven Roberts?"

His head tilts. "Yes..."

"You don't know me, but my name is Jess." I don't give him my last name for now. "I'm sorry for showing up unannounced like this, but if it wouldn't be too much trouble, might I take a few minutes of your time?"

Great. I sound like a solicitor trying to sell him something.

He must pick up the same vibe, because he shakes his head as he starts to close the door. "Sorry, I'm not interested."

In an act of desperation, I blurt, "Lily. Does Lily live here? Perhaps I can talk to her?"

This gets his attention. The blue in his eyes sharpens with alarm, his brow furrowing. "You know my wife?"

"Well, I don't *know* her exactly, but—"

"Lily... she's dead."

CHAPTER SIXTEEN

I STAND THERE, THE RINGING IN MY EARS FADING OUT, STARING AT him with my mouth open. "She... died?"

I suppose that explains why the letters stopped and why there was never any legal action pursued against Catherine.

"A long time ago." He stares at his socked feet on the foyer wood, rubbing his arm.

"I'm so sorry to hear that."

His eyes brush over me with a glint of suspicion. "If you were a friend of hers, you would have known that. Who did you say you were again?"

I lick my lips and wring my hands. I need to find a way to keep his attention. "My mother-in-law was a friend of Lily's."

"Did she send you here?"

"No," I admit. "It's complicated."

He frowns. "Is that why you're here? Because it's complicated?"

"Yes. Well, I—I'm hoping you can help me with something."

He studies me a moment more. "All right."

"I promise it won't take long."

For the first time since he opened the door, his demeanor softens, and he steps aside. "Would you like to come in for a few minutes? I was just about to make some coffee." He sighs. "It would be nice to have company. The house gets lonely."

I nod and take a deep breath. "Yes, I'll come in for a minute."

"I'm interested to know what you know about Lily," he says, closing the door behind me.

"My mother-in-law was the one who knew her." I rub my temple. "I... well, I came across some letters from her."

He leads me into the kitchen, where a few white appliances out on the counter match the rest of the room. It's tidy. Nothing is out of place, and it smells faintly of cleaning products. We head over to a breakfast nook with a round light-pine table with a newspaper sitting in the center. I know what's missing now—a feminine touch. I look at him as he's pouring the coffee into the two mugs and get a dull ache of sadness for him.

"I'm recently married," I say. "I can't imagine what you're going through. Losing your wife."

Steven rubs the gray scruff across his jawline. "Lily's been gone a long time. But some days are harder than others."

"I'm sure it's not something you ever get fully used to, even after a long time has passed."

He shrugs, his smile nostalgic. "No, but it does get easier." He looks at me, brows knitting. "You said your mother-in-law knew Lily? Why didn't she come with you?"

"Well, to be honest, she doesn't know I'm here."

"Oh?"

"I found something in her basement that worried me a bit. I wanted to talk to you first, without my mother-in-law knowing. I hope that's not a problem."

He leans forward, and his chair squeaks. "It must have

been important for you to come all this way to visit a man you don't know."

"You're right. It is that important," I admit.

He listens politely as the words tumble out, and I tell him all about the letters I found in the basement. His eyes widen. When I'm finished with my explanation, Steven sits there quietly, rubbing his stubble, a concentrated expression on his face. I see the full-scale weight of what misery and suffering can do to a person. It's like a stain in his eyes, an inkblot, unable to be undone or washed away.

"I told you Lily died, but I didn't say how," he says finally.

A nervous sensation travels across the back of my neck like the whisper of a ghost.

"Okay..."

Steven presses his palm to the table. He's still wearing his gold wedding ring. "Lily took her own life."

I swallow down the knot in my throat. "She did?"

He raises his eyes, and gloom stares back at me. "After our son, Freddy, died, she had a psychotic break. She just couldn't handle it. She went off the deep end. I tried to get her help and get her to go to therapy. She agreed to attend a couple of sessions, but nothing seemed to be working. The doctor prescribed her antidepressants, but she refused to take them. She said she wasn't depressed or crazy. She said she knew in her heart that Freddy wasn't her real son. I guess one day she just couldn't take it anymore, when no one would believe her." He pauses. His eyes are red rimmed. "She killed herself. I take responsibility. I had no idea she would be capable of something like that. I knew she was sick, but..." He raises his gaze to the ceiling, his chin trembling, and draws in a shaky breath. "I failed her."

I sit six inches from this stranger, in his kitchen, his eyes glassy with tears, his face wrinkled in grief. When he returns his gaze to his lap, a few rogue tears spill over and roll down his cheeks, a physical mark of what loss can do to a person.

"Had she ever talked about suicide before?" I ask, my head reeling with this new development.

Steven traces a groove in the pine with his index finger and says nothing. His eyelashes are damp.

"I'm sorry," I begin again. "I don't mean to show up on your doorstep like this, asking you to relive painful memories of your dead wife. That's not what this is at all. It's just—well—I told you about what was in those letters. They frightened me. She sounded so distraught, almost to the point of being traumatized."

"She *was* distraught. Freddy's death changed her, unlocked this darkness inside her. Like you say, it could have traumatized her."

"That didn't happen to you, though," I point out.

Steven sniffs, still looking at the table. "People respond differently to heartbreak. They grieve in different ways."

"But this is more than just grieving. She accused Catherine, my mother-in-law, of swapping her baby with yours in the hospital. Her words were powerful. She really thought, whether true or not, that Catherine stole her baby."

Steven shakes his head as if to erase the past. "Lily plunged into this deep darkness. She let it swallow her whole. She was so far gone. None of us could reach her."

"What do you mean 'none of us'?"

His finger goes to work on the groove in the wood again. "Friends, doctors, family."

"So there *were* people trying to help her?"

"To a certain degree, yes. She was uncooperative for the most part. She just kept insisting that we needed to believe her, that her baby was stolen at birth and Freddy was this other woman's baby."

"Did you know she was sending all these letters?" I unzip my purse and pull out my phone to show him the photographs I took in the basement. "Was this her handwriting?"

"Yes, it looks exactly like the way she wrote."

He shakes his head again and pinches the bridge of his nose with his thumb and forefinger. Then he pushes the phone away. "Sorry, I just need a second."

"No, I'm the one who should be apologizing to you." Guilt gushes through me. "You didn't ask for these memories to be drummed up out of nowhere. But like I said, I'm married to the man who might have been the abducted child all those years ago. He has no idea. I don't know what to do—if I should tell him, if I should let it go, or whether it still makes a difference. It was just so shocking to find those letters. I didn't come here to upset you. I came here to get answers." I wipe a tear from my cheek, moved by this man and his memories. "Can I ask... did you or your wife ever have a DNA test to check that Freddy was definitely your son?"

Steven's eyelashes are wet when he opens them and looks at me. He takes a deep breath. "No. Lily mentioned it a few times, but I always said no. Freddy was born with a heart defect. We always knew his time with us could be short. But he also went to many doctors' appointments, and we all had the same blood type. That was enough for me."

I nod. I think I see fear in Steven's expression. It could be that he didn't want to believe Lily could be right. I can't say I would accept a blood type as proof, given the circumstances, but perhaps I'm biased by the letters I found. Steven clearly didn't suspect Catherine of any foul play.

"Do you remember Catherine from the hospital when Freddy was born?" I ask.

"Yes. She was a sweet woman who chatted with Lily a

lot." He pauses. "But I didn't like the husband. He was very... stern."

"Do you remember anything more about them?" I ask.

He shakes his head. "Sorry, no. I think Catherine and Lily stayed in touch after."

"Yeah, I gleaned that from the letters," I say. "Mark and Freddy were friends for a time."

The thought makes me feel incredibly sad. *What if Lily was right, and her son was right there under her nose?*

"Can you tell me a little about your wife's mental state after Freddy died?" I ask.

Steven nods, his eyes blank, staring at nothing. "It was a terrible time."

"You don't have to talk about it if you don't want to."

He takes a deep breath and continues, struggling with the words at first, but then his voice smooths out, and he gets into a rhythm, explaining what it was like.

"Freddy was our only child. Lily lost all sense of reality after he passed away. At first, it was these subtle things she would say."

"Like what?"

"She would make comments, vague, randomly. Saying things like Freddy was never her son. I thought it was just part of her grieving process, that she was in shock. But things just got worse instead of better."

"How?"

"Even when Freddy was alive, she would say things like 'He's sickly. He doesn't look like us. He can't be our son. Something must have happened in the hospital.' Then after he died, she just spiraled to a point at which there was nothing any of us could to do to improve her mental state."

"I'm so sorry you have had to deal with all this on top of

losing both your wife and son." *What else can a person say to someone who has experienced such significant loss?*

He raises his damp eyelashes. "I'm sorry, but I don't think it's good idea for you to be here anymore. I don't mean to be rude, but I'm having a difficult time..." He stares at the wall.

I nod and stand, prepared to leave him be, upset at myself for disrupting his Saturday morning. But then a thought occurs to me.

"I'm so sorry to put you through pain you're trying to heal from. It can be agony, opening old wounds. But can I ask you one last question?"

He's walking me out of the kitchen now, escorting me down the hall toward his front door.

"Sure." He sniffs.

I unlock my phone and swipe through my camera roll to pull up a picture of Mark. In it, he's a toddler, sitting next to a tabby cat with a big grin on his face. I took the photo from one of the albums Catherine showed me.

"This is my husband, Mark, when he was a child." I flick across to a picture of him as an adult. "Do you see anything in him you might recognize from your past?"

Steven stops abruptly. His eyes land on the picture of Mark, widening. His jaw slackens. He looks from the picture to me then back again.

"Wait right here. I'll be right back."

He hurries down the hall. There's an urgency in his movements. He turns the corner, disappearing into a part of the house I can no longer see.

CHAPTER SEVENTEEN

Steven shuffles back down the hallway and emerges around the corner carrying a navy photo album with gold trim around the spine. He's out of breath by the time he stops beside me and flicks through the pages. We stand there, our arms almost touching. The plastic protector crinkles as his finger moves steadily across the page. I can tell he's searching for something in particular.

"Here." He pushes his finger against the plastic protector. "This. Look here."

My jaw drops. "That picture looks just like Mark—well, the way he looks in his baby pictures."

Steven shakes his head. "These are *my* baby pictures."

I gawk at him, pointing now too. "That's you in these pictures? Not your son, Freddy?"

"No." He's still shaking his head. "That's me."

"You look… *exactly* like Mark in these pictures. Your eyes, the shape of your nose, your hair color… it's like looking at a reflection of him."

Something sour swirls inside my stomach. Steven meets my gaze, and our eyes lock. There's recognition in his eyes, not familiar recognition, but a mutual agreement that something isn't right, that the terrible words in Lily's letters could really be the awful truth.

A light rises in his eyes as if he's having an epiphany. I'm watching in real time a person coming to terms with the idea that certain parts of his life might have been a lie.

"I'm so sorry," I whisper because I can't manage to find my regular voice.

Steven's eyes flutter back down to the picture of him as a child. He's sitting on a rocking horse, gripping the handles and wearing a cloth diaper pinned with bobby pins. Now that I'm studying it harder, I see that everything about the picture is vintage. He's wearing a dark-green shirt that's one size too small. Orange shag carpet is in the background along with a brick fireplace with an antique-looking gold or brass fire poker behind him in a basket. He's grinning from ear to ear, as if whoever took the picture told him to give a big smile for the camera.

"Let me see that picture again of your husband," Steven says softly, his eyes still focused on his own baby picture.

I pull it up on my phone and hold it up next to the picture of Steven. We both slowly raise our heads and stare at each other.

Steven licks his lips, his eyes wide with shock and disbelief.

"Was she right?" he asks not to me in particular but more to himself, his eyes glazed over with confusion.

"Do you have any others? Any of you when you're a little older so we can compare those?"

He starts plowing through the pages, going toward the back of the book.

"Here's one. I was going to get my Eagle Scout that day. That's why I'm dressed in the Boy Scout uniform."

I don't have to scrutinize the picture to know that this one looks even more like Mark. The jaw structure, cheekbones, eye shape, eye color, and hair color are almost identical to Mark's.

"This is unbelievable," I say, holding up the picture of Mark on my phone again to compare.

He takes a step backward, his palm pressed to his forehead.

"Steven..."

Whatever I've done, there's no undoing it now.

His big gray eyes slice through me. "Will you email me that picture of your husband?"

I stare at him, gulping.

"Please?"

"Sure—yes. Yes, I'll do it now."

Steven looks relieved and gives me his email address. I type it into my phone and attach the picture of Mark. Steven checks his phone, confirming the receipt with a nod.

"Do you mind if I take a picture of this picture?" I point at the one where Steven's standing outside of a building, his shoulders straight, a proud half smile on his face. He's handsome, going places, the whole world in front of him, just like Mark is now. It's an overwhelming realization that this man in the picture, the one standing beside me, could be his real father.

It's hitting Steven hard too. "All this time, was she really right? Did our baby get abducted, *switched* at birth? Could something like that have even really happened?" He shakes his head sadly and lets out a low moan.

"Maybe it would have been easier to get away with back then," I say. "It was thirty years ago. They didn't have the same rules and regulations in place. They didn't have to match the baby's hospital bracelet with the mother's and scan it like they do now."

Steven presses his palm to his head again as if to contain all the morbid thoughts going through his brain.

"I-I can't believe this," he stammers, his eyes still wide as he stares blankly ahead.

"I'm going to go ahead and take the picture if you don't mind." I take one of the whole picture then zoom into his face. While Steven stands there like a zombie, I flip back to the rocking horse picture and snap a photo of that one too. Then I set the album on the foyer table.

Steven looks at me. "What are you going to do with the pictures?"

"I don't know yet. What about you for the one I sent you?"

Steven mechanically shakes his head. "I have no idea. I need time to process all this."

"I have your email now, and you have mine. We can be in touch," I say. "Mark is in Japan right now. He works at an insurance company, and they needed him there for a new client. He comes home in four or five weeks, and we can decide then." I consider Catherine for a moment. "I'm not sure how to handle my mother-in-law."

"Jeez. Could she really have stolen my son?"

I place a hand on his arm, trying to calm him. "We can't know that for sure. There may have been a mix-up at the hospital."

"Right," he says, his eyes unfocused. "What a mess. You will be in touch, won't you? I don't think I can go on just living my life knowing that... that my Lily might have been right." Steven looks at me, his jaw slack and his pupils as wide as saucers.

"I promise," I say.

Steven walks me out, waits for me to get in my Uber, then

watches as we drive away. I stare at him through the rearview mirror until the driver turns down a different street. Steven and his house disappear. I'm not sure I'll ever forget the look in his eyes—the realization and horror.

On the ride back to Catherine's house, I brainstorm ways in which to drop this bombshell on Mark. This life-altering, web-of-deceit information will change the course of everything.

I have no idea how he'll react or how Catherine will react. I feel like I still need more proof that it was intentional and not an accident.

I take a deep breath. The Uber driver's eyes meet mine in the rearview mirror, and I quickly look away. So I watch the houses blur around me, a sick feeling in the pit of my stomach. It gets worse when he pulls into the driveway. I'm going to have to tell Mark who he really is. I just don't know how or when.

My palms are clammy as I thank the driver and open the car door. My legs are sludge as I make my way up the steps leading to this creepy house, which always seems like it's alive, watching me, breathing, waiting for me to make a critical mistake and offering me no help whatsoever. It's just cold drafts, dark hallways, and a mother-in-law harboring a terrible secret.

CHAPTER EIGHTEEN

I walk through the front door to find Catherine waiting halfway between the window and the door. She crosses her arms, her eyes shimmering like icicles. A shiver jolts up my spine.

"Catherine." I halt in my tracks, breathless and temporarily immobilized by the anger in her face.

"Where. Have. You. Been?" She takes one step in my direction, each word clipped, like a strike from a venomous snake.

I recoil from her, backing toward the wall. "I... I went out," I stammer, taken off guard.

"Where?"

"Just out. I wanted to get out of the house for a little while."

"You don't have any bags. You didn't go shopping? Didn't run errands? How did you get out?" Her voice is an accusatory screech.

"I—a driver—Uber—I took an Uber." I swallow hard, unprepared for this ambush, my brain racing to come up with an answer on the spot.

"So you think it's okay to just leave, unannounced, and take off without telling me?"

I clamp my mouth shut, frowning at her, thinking. She has no right to speak to me this way. I'm a guest in her home. She's not my mother. She may not even be Mark's mother.

"Catherine." I hold out my hand to stop her from coming any closer because she's trying to inch her way forward. I can tell she wants to get in my face, the fuel in her eyes burning through me. It's like her stare is trying to get through the back of my brain, to pluck out each individual lie. All I can do is remain calm and give her vague answers to try to satisfy her. "I just went out for a little bit. I don't have to tell you where I've been. You're not my keeper."

"If you wanted fresh air, I've told you a million times you can just go walk around the grounds."

I wish my ankle were healed so I could drive away from this woman right now. I feel chained to this house, to Catherine and her ridiculous rules.

"There are times when I just want to walk around the town or the park. I want to see other people and feel like I'm still part of society—"

"You have a broken ankle, and you want to *walk*?" she snaps. "You should be resting so that it heals!"

"I can take a stroll," I say, exasperated. "It's hard for me to be here, Catherine. I'm used to a bigger city. You have to understand that and give me time to adjust. All I have right now is the house, you, and work. I need more. I'm not being stimulated enough, not getting enough exercise. I wish you could understand that and try not to take it personally. If you were so worried about where I was, you could have just called or texted me."

Catherine's bottom lip juts out like she's a pouting child

not getting her way. Her arms remain tightly locked around her chest.

"Would you have even answered if I did that?"

"Yes, of course."

"I don't know if I believe that. You don't seem to want me around," she says, her voice high and whining.

"Again, don't take it personally. I don't think it's healthy for us to spend every waking moment together."

"Well, I *do* take it personally. It's like you don't want to be here with me, that you want to get away from me any chance you get. You act like I'm glued to your hip! It's simply not true."

"Please don't put words in my mouth. It's not like that at all. Besides, I thought it would be okay because you weren't even home when I left. I had no idea when you would be back. I didn't want to be in the house alone."

"Well, join the club!" Catherine exclaims. "Now you know how I feel. Anyway, you are contradicting yourself. You say you need space from me but don't want to be alone here."

"The house is dark. It makes noises that freak me out sometimes. I want to get away. It has nothing to do with you."

"You don't like my house either now?" she scoffs.

"I didn't say that."

"Well, you're certainly implying it."

I take a deep breath, backtracking. "I'll try to take your feelings into consideration from now on, but Catherine, you've really gotta try to meet me in the middle here and do the same for me."

Her brow knits. "What do you mean?"

"You have to give me space. You can't be hanging all over me, demanding to know where I am every little second of the day. It's... suffocating. If I don't want to be in the house, it doesn't mean I don't *like* the house. I just don't want to be in it sometimes."

Her cheeks and neck blotch with patches of red. She looks away, uncrosses her arms, and throws them to the ceiling. "Excuse me for trying to be available and making my large home accommodating to you."

"I understand all that. I'm just trying to tell you that I'm a grown woman. I can come and go as I please."

Catherine makes a huffing noise. "Then do it. I won't stand in your way." She dramatically rolls her wrist, spins on a heel, and marches off into the living room.

I sigh and walk up the stairs, holding the railing, my boot feeling heavier than ever. Every part of my body feels heavier than ever. I'm carrying the weight of knowing what I know along with dealing with Catherine's bizarre outbursts. When I get to my room, I collapse onto the bed face down, my sweaty skin finally cooled by the bed linens. And that's where I stay for a while, trying to quiet my racing thoughts.

A couple of hours later, Catherine knocks lightly on my door. Her delicate voice floats through the wood. "Jess, I want to apologize for my behavior earlier. I was out of line." She pauses, expecting me to reply. I don't. Then she continues, "I made dinner for us. Your favorite, grilled salmon and baked potatoes. I would love it if you'd join me. We can have a glass of chardonnay on the back deck to take the edge off and relax."

I wait a beat. Her personality changes are an emotional roller coaster, but I call out anyway, "Okay. Thanks."

I walk to the door and open it, but Catherine is no longer standing on the other side. I glance down the hallway left, then right, frowning. *How did she disappear so fast?*

Slowly and steadily, I hobble down the stairs. The aroma of grilled salmon wafts through the air before I get to the kitchen, making my stomach grumble. Catherine is setting the table outside. I open the back door and cast her a wave and a smile I hope she finds sincere enough to repair the frayed tapestry between us.

"You came down." Catherine's eyes sparkle with delight.

"Of course. You had me at salmon. Thank you for apologizing. Maybe we both overreacted. I shouldn't have said the things I said either."

She bats a hand. "No, darling, I was out of line, just like you said." She pushes my seat out for me and gestures for me to fill it. "I will be better from now on. I promise. I just worry about you. That's all."

"Worry about me? Why?"

Catherine fills my wineglass halfway.

"All mothers worry" is all she says.

I don't ask her to elaborate. I sit there, chewing my food and making banal conversation.

"It's a beautiful evening," she says. "Where did you go for your walk earlier?"

"A park," I say, searching through my mind for the name of a local park to use. "Eddington Park."

"How lovely," she says. "Is the duck pond still there?"

I smile. "Yes."

A corner of Catherine's lips rises, but she doesn't say anything more.

After dinner, I help her clear the table, but I'm not feeling well. Exhaustion from the day hits me out of nowhere. I yawn and blink my burning eyes and tell Catherine I am going upstairs to lie down.

"I'll take care of the rest of the dishes, darling. Don't worry about it." Her voice is dripping honey.

I climb the stairs again and trudge down the hallway, barely able to keep my eyes open. After laying my head on my pillow, I succumb to the haze of fatigue wrapped around me like a cape within minutes.

CHAPTER NINETEEN

I peel one eye open then the other. The world is just a blur of wooly-looking shapes. Something dark is moving on the other side of the room. I can't make sense of its shape.

"Hello?" I rasp then clear my throat and try again, but my voice still sounds like I'm gargling with gravel.

I try to sit up, but my head is pounding like a jackhammer. I clutch the sides, and a throbbing shoots across my forehead before traveling to the back of my skull. Even the tiniest glimpse of light causes agony. I squeeze my eyes shut and suck in a sharp breath. When I open them a few seconds later, everything is still blurry.

My mouth tastes like pennies, and my tongue is gritty, as if it's made of sandpaper. I glance at my bedside table and groan. There's no water glass, nothing to quench my extreme thirst.

I try to swing my legs over the side of the bed. I'm still dressed in my clothes from last night. Then I hear a thumping noise on the other side of the room, as if someone hit the side of the dresser.

I whip my head around, which makes me dizzy and nauseated.

"Is someone in here?" I croak.

No response comes. I knead my sore eyes with my palms and blink, trying again. But I don't see anything. That's weird. I could have sworn I saw a moving blurry shape when I first opened my eyes. *And what was that bumping noise?* My eyes and ears are playing tricks on me, and I don't like it. This seems different somehow than the usual creaks and moans of the house. This was someone or something in my room. I'm sure of it.

My door is open too.

"Who's there?" I squeak. "Catherine? I'm really thirsty. Are you there? My head hurts. Something's wrong."

The jackhammer continues nailing the back of my skull, the pain reverberating down my shoulders and spine. My stomach is churning. My mouth fills with saliva. If I'm going to be sick, I need to get to the bathroom before the contents of my stomach come spraying out all over the floor.

I manage to stand up and start hobbling to the bathroom, but I trip over my boot. My knees slam into the wood floor, making my breath leave my lungs. I can't draw any more in. Pain surges through me like someone is pounding a gong inside me.

I fall forward, smacking the side of my face on the edge of the bedpost. Everything goes black.

* * *

I grasp for consciousness, teetering on the edge, but my brain won't let me wake up. Vivid images fill my mind, and I don't know if they're lucid dreams or reality. I can't make sense of anything that's happening.

A voice is whispering in my ear, and I realize I'm being dragged. I smell the faint scent of lavender and maybe a hint of something stronger like peppermint.

My teeth chatter, and my bones ache, as if I'm sick with a fever. The front of my head is sore, but the incessant drilling pain has stopped. Soft laughter tinkles, and someone speaks in a low voice, as if they're deliberately trying to be quiet. My eyelids flutter, my eyes working overtime underneath them, but I can't seem to pry them open.

My body is strangely still during all this, as if I've succumbed to some sort of weird sleep paralysis, even though nothing like that has ever happened to me before. I start to panic in my dream or in the reality, whatever it is. I'm trapped somewhere in between. I try to move my frozen body. *Why am I so cold?* A warm light makes me squint under my closed eyelids, but I continue trying to open them, unable to escape from the dizzy haze that's keeping them sealed shut.

I start to cry, but I can't tell if it's only happening in my dream. My cheeks feel damp.

Then I drift back into a deeper unconsciousness, succumbing to a severe fatigue that has a chokehold on my body.

I don't know how much time has passed when I'm finally able to open my eyes. I stir in my bed. My headache is not as sharp as it was before.

When I blink away the fogginess from my vision, the shape of Catherine forms beside my bed. She's sitting beside me. My eyelids flutter the rest of the way open.

"Where am I?" I croak.

Catherine's voice is a melodic lullaby. "You're in your bed, darling."

"What happened? Were you in my room before? Were you laughing?"

Catherine frowns and tilts her head to the side, studying me as if I'm a difficult math problem she can't work out. "Laughing? No. I heard a thud and came to check on you. Honey, you had a bad fall, so I helped you back into bed."

"I swear I heard laughter." I lick my lips, still parched, and bring my hand up to my forehead to rub some of the soreness away, but I wince in pain and quickly draw my hand away.

"Careful, now. You have a nasty bruise on your forehead."

"That explains the pain," I groan.

Catherine nods, her eyes shimmering with sympathy. "I put an ice pack on it while you were sleeping. It's helped bring some of the swelling down a bit, but it's going to leave a bruise for a little while, I'm afraid."

I smack my lips. "I'm so thirsty."

Catherine reaches toward the edge of my bedside table and lifts a glass of water, helps me sit up, then brings it to my lips. I lap at like a thirsty dog, gulping it down.

Catherine removes it, all but prying it from my lips. She gives me a solemn shake of her head and casts me a reprimanding look. "You don't want to make yourself sick by drinking too much at once."

"Please," I whine.

"You can have more in a moment." She sets the glass back down.

"How did I fall?"

"I don't know. I heard a thud and came running. I found you unconscious on the floor. You wouldn't respond to commands. You were limp."

I shake my head and wince, remembering the scorching pain. Something about this story doesn't make sense.

"You came immediately after you heard the thud?"

"Yes."

"And you said I was unconscious? What did I hit my head on?"

"I'm assuming the side of your bed."

I vaguely recall this, but the memory is murky.

"Why didn't you call for an ambulance to take me to the hospital if I was knocked unconscious from a head injury?"

Instead of giving me an answer, Catherine opens her clasped hands, which are sitting in her lap. In it are two oblong pills, tiny, but I can't read what they say. They're the capsule kind.

She lifts my glass of water again and tries to part my lips with her fingers.

I shake my head and clamp my mouth shut, squirming. "What? No. Catherine. I should go to the hospital to be checked out."

"Just take this medicine. You'll be fine, darling. You're awake now, aren't you?"

"Yeah, but I could have a concussion or something. I can't believe you didn't call for an ambulance or take me in to get checked out when I was unconscious and unresponsive. Head injuries can be very serious."

Catherine's eyes narrow, darkening a shade.

"You don't *need* a hospital. I am perfectly capable of taking care of you, and I'm offering you medicine to help you feel better."

"I'm not taking that." I point at the pills sitting in her open palm. "I don't even know what it is."

"It's pain medication."

"Pain medication makes me feel funny. I don't like it. Never have."

"It will also help with the swelling," she says.

I make sure to meet her gaze and hold eye contact when I say as firmly as I can, "No."

Suddenly desperate to get out of this bed, I sit up straight. I toss the sheets off my legs, but when I try to swing them over the side of the bed, they weigh a ton. I groan and plop down on the pillow, staring up at the ceiling. I'm going nowhere anytime soon. My body feels like it's been dipped into a vat of concrete, and now it's dripping off me, solidifying more and more every moment.

"Just rest, darling. It's the best thing for you right now." Catherine brings her hand up to stroke my cheek, but I jerk away from her touch.

She draws her hand back, her face shattering with hurt. "You don't trust me."

"I don't know what to think right now." My voice cracks, and I choke back a sob, staring at the ceiling, partly because I don't want to look at her and partly because if I don't, the tears are going to spill over the sides of my face. I don't want to cry in front of her. I've already shown enough weakness. The sobs are there, though, waiting in my chest, demanding to explode.

Catherine stands up. "I'll make you some warm broth."

"I'm not hungry."

Catherine says nothing, just walks away, leaving the door open as she enters the hallway. After she disappears, I glance around for my phone. If I can call another taxi and get out of here, I'll head to the first hotel or bed-and-breakfast I can find. But I can barely lift my head, much less walk anywhere. For now, I'm stuck with Catherine and her overbearing need to coddle me.

It's like all the energy in my bones has been sucked out, leaving me drained and depleted so that I can't fend for myself.

A torturous need to sleep engulfs me again, swallowing

me whole. I close my eyes, wondering if she put something in the water.

CHAPTER TWENTY

When I wake, blinking away the haze of sleep, I slowly become aware of my surroundings. Catherine is by my side again, sitting on the edge of my bed, and every muscle in my body tenses. She gently strokes my arm as I recoil from her.

Catherine sighs. "You need to drink."

She brings the water glass to my lips again, and I'm too thirsty to argue, so I open my mouth and guzzle it down. I try to take the glass a couple of times, but Catherine backs it away, swatting gently at my hand.

"No, darling. I need to help you," she insists.

"I can do it myself."

"No, you can't."

"It's dripping down my chin. Please."

Catherine relents with another sigh, as if I'm the one putting her out and not the other way around.

I wipe my chin with the back of my hand and take another swallow. Catherine clasps her hand over mine and gives it a squeeze. My knuckles dent into her palm. I stiffen. She either doesn't notice or pretends not to.

"How are you feeling?" Catherine asks in her usual honey voice.

"A little better."

"That's good." She strokes my cheek.

"My head still hurts."

"I offered you medicine when you were awake last time. Do you want it this time?"

"No, thank you."

"Are you sure? It will make you feel better."

I shake my head again and pinch my lips together, trying not to cry. The tears betray me. flooding my eyes anyway.

"Shh," she whispers, stroking under my cheekbone with her thumb, wiping the unruly tears away. "Don't cry, darling."

I sniffle, staring at the window, feeling the quiver in my chin, and wishing Mark were here—wishing I were anywhere but here. I want my husband. I want to get out of this house. *Who the fuck is this woman? Just how batshit is she?* Nausea turns my stomach, and pain thunders between my temples. Exhaustion creeps over my body, and I begin to wonder.

What did she put in the water? Do I feel this sick because she drugged me? Or because I hit my head on the furniture? I'm not sure which is worse. I could have some sort of traumatic brain injury. There could be swelling underneath my skull. There's no way for me to tell because Catherine won't take me to get checked out.

"What's wrong, darling?" she asks.

"Catherine, I need to go to a hospital. I don't feel well. I feel sick."

She strokes my hair. "Do you need me to help you to the bathroom?"

I shake my head, but the movement hurts. "If you won't take me to a doctor, then leave me alone."

"If you need me to take you to the bathroom, I will," she says.

"I'll be fine." I take a deep breath to rein in some of the nausea. It helps a little. "Just leave me alone."

Catherine stands, her shoulders straight, her jaw clenched. "Suit yourself, then."

She strides from the room, this time closing the door behind her.

The moment she's gone, I instinctively reach for the bedside table for my phone, but my fingers scrape across the wood surface and come up empty. I try the drawer, but it's also empty. The charger I usually leave there is gone too. I sit up straighter, my heart pounding against my ribcage and adrenaline surging through my veins.

My fingers fumble through the sheets as I search for my phone, lifting the linens and tossing them away. I grab my pillow and shake it, but my phone is nowhere. Wincing, I swing my legs over the side again. This time I'm successful, and my feet hit solid ground.

I notice for the first time that I'm wearing a pair of pink jogger shorts and a white tank top. I don't remember dressing myself in this. Catherine did it. God only knows what else she's done. I wouldn't put it past her to have bathed me or something while I was unconscious.

I need to get the hell out of here while I still have a chance. I'm done being a pawn in her sick and twisted little game. I get down on my hands and knees, checking under the bed to see if my phone accidentally fell under it.

It's not there.

Terror fills every cell in my body when I realize I can't find my laptop either. It's not on the bed beside me, where I last remember having it.

Frantically, I comb through the room and the bathroom,

searching even the most ridiculous areas, like behind the toilet or in the shower. They're gone. My laptop and my phone are *gone*.

Catherine must have taken them.

I hobble to the door, filled with fury. But when I clutch the doorknob, I discover that it is now locked—from the outside.

There's no breaking out of these old doors. The wood is an inch thick. I run my fingers over the lock. Maybe I could remove it if I had a screwdriver and some basic knowledge of home repair, but I don't.

I grit my teeth and trudge to the window. But of course, it's painted shut. I look down. Even if I *could* somehow manage to get out of this window, it would be a straight-down drop, at least twenty feet, maybe more. And that's with a partially healed broken ankle.

The panic is rising now. Catherine has taken my phone and locked me in this room, and she might even be drugging me. The nausea is gone. My instincts sharpen, but the brain fog won't clear. Pulling in a deep breath to calm myself, I head to the bathroom, where I dump out the contents of my makeup bag, trying to find something small enough to push through the tiny hole in the doorknob. *If I can get it open somehow with something small enough...*

All I can find is a set of tweezers. I have no idea what I'm doing, but it doesn't hurt to try. I limp back to the door with them in my fist. Then I jam them into the slit, but the tweezers are slightly too big.

I groan in frustration and throw the tweezers at the door. Back to square one, I search the entire room for something smaller—a bobby pin, a safety pin, anything at this point. There's nothing in this godforsaken room that's narrow enough to squeeze through the little hole.

Instead, I beat my hands against the wood. "Catherine! Let me out of here! Let me out!"

That's when my mother-in-law's cackling laughter fills my ears. I'm breathing heavily, leaning against the door. She's laughing at me. I can't believe it.

I press my palm to the door then slam it down once, twice, harder, faster each time.

"Let me out of here right now! What are you doing? Are you crazy?"

"I'm not *crazy*," Catherine barks, her laughter tranquilized in an instant.

The change in her tone makes my body jolt with shock, like there's ice in my veins.

"Please let me out," I say, this time keeping my tone polite. "I'm so sorry if I have offended you in some way or—"

"You are being so silly," she says. Her voice is back to its usual sweetness.

"Silly?" I shake my head. "But you locked me in here."

"I'm doing what's best for you."

"How?"

"You should learn not to be so stubborn." She clucks her tongue.

"Catherine, stop this," I plead. "If you let me out now, I'll never tell a soul what happened. I promise I won't tell Mark."

"Not until you get some much-needed rest," she says.

I rest my head against the door, exhaustion taking away any of the energy I had left. "This isn't funny anymore."

"No one said it was funny," she retorts.

"Why are you doing this?"

"Because you won't listen." I can hear the smirk in her tone.

"Unlock this door or else," I say through gritted teeth.

"Or else what?" Catherine's voice is a springtime meadow, cool, breezy, and innocent.

"Or else..." I glance around the room, looking for something I could either use as a weapon or to defend myself with. "I'll hurt you." The words die in my throat. I don't have anything to attack her with, and my boot won't get me far very fast.

The door clicks then opens slowly. Catherine takes a single step inside. Her eyes are dark and cold, her expression evil. The barrel of a pistol is pointed at me, looming, warning. She's steady, not a single shake of her hand or the gun.

I stumble back, my jaw dropping, and Catherine takes another step into the room, the gun in her hand heavy, cold steel aimed directly at my face.

CHAPTER TWENTY-ONE

Catherine's eyes glint in the soft morning glow. The gun seems out of place in this room filled with sunshine. "I'm sorry for having to use extreme measures to get you to rest and do what I'm asking you. But you have to learn some way, don't you?"

I stand frozen in fear, my heart rattling, my legs watery. "Catherine, I—"

"That's enough!" she snaps, her voice ricocheting off the walls. "Stop talking. Just *stop*."

Inside my brain, the same words bounce around over and over again. *This can't be happening. This isn't real. My mother-in-law is not pointing a gun at my face. But she is. It's real. And now I have to comply with her commands if I want to live.*

"Catherine," I begin again. "Please calm down."

"Go to the bed." She pushes the pistol in the direction of the bed then points it back toward me. "Now."

I walk backward, not wanting to take my eyes off her for a single second. When I get to the edge, I stop.

"Now get in." Her cold eyes meet mine. There's nothing left of the sweet woman I once knew.

Complying, I slowly climb into the bed. "Why are you doing this to me?"

Catherine doesn't give me an answer to that question. Instead, she says, every word dripping malice, "Now, you are going to *stay* in that bed until I say otherwise."

How do you reason with someone pointing a gun at your face? I'm having trouble wrapping my head around why she is doing this, but then a thought dawns on me, screaming to the front of my brain.

She must know. She *has* to somehow have found out that I was snooping on her. Maybe she has hidden cameras in the house somewhere. She's not very tech savvy, but she could have hired someone to do it for her.

The realization hits me like a ton of bricks. She wants my silence. That's why she stole my phone, so I can't tell Mark about what I found.

"Please don't kill me." Tears slide down my face as I whimper out the words in despair.

Catherine shakes her head. "I'm not... I'm not going to *kill* you."

But she doesn't sound sure. She sounds like someone who hasn't thought through what she's going to do next.

A million scenarios whirl through my brain. *How could Catherine know I found the letters?* I wonder if she followed me when I went to Steven's house. Or she figured out the passcode to my phone and saw the pictures and the emails with Steven. I swallow down the bile rising in my throat, trying to put on a front of bravery, of innocence, and not the panic skewering me.

Catherine starts backing toward the door with the gun still aimed steadily at me.

"Where are you going?"

"Stop talking." Catherine's jaw is tight, each word a dagger.

I freeze, staring between the barrel of the gun and her.

She backs toward the door again, her pace a crawl. She keeps the gun pointed at me, not even flitting her eyes away, but they're pooling with tears now, and her nostrils are flaring.

"I wanted to do something nice for you," she says, "but you ruined it. You took away any chance of us ever being close. You should have known better."

I swallow hard and don't question her, even though inside my head, I'm screaming to know what she means, to decipher what this torture is all about.

Catherine steps out of the door, but she orders me not to move. I stay frozen, like the two blocks of ice that are her eyes.

She bends down and picks something up from the floor, careful to keep the gun raised and aimed. When she straightens, she's holding a plate. On that plate is a sandwich cut in half.

I swallow hard and stare at her.

"What... what are you doing?"

"I told you to stop talking, Jess. You're wasting your breath." She sets the sandwich down on the bedside table. "I'm leaving now. You need to eat something. It will be good for your stomach. Trust me. Even though I know you don't trust me, which is exactly why we're in this situation in the first place."

She's right. I don't trust her, and I'm certainly not going to eat or drink anything she brings me. I swallow down the words I want to yell in her face and behave as if I'm ready to comply.

And I don't ask her about the laptop and the phone either.

It's no use. She won't give them to me even if I ask. I'll have to think of a way of manipulating her into giving them back.

Catherine reaches behind her and pulls something shiny and metal out of her back pocket. I stiffen and sit up straighter in the bed when I see it's a pair of handcuffs.

"Give me your wrist," she demands.

I don't move.

"Now." Catherine's eyes bore into mine. Then she shakes the gun, and I flinch but don't give up my wrist.

She pushes her thumb against the safety catch on the gun, and it makes a clicking sound.

I inhale a sharp breath. "All right." With my hand shaking, I raise my arm.

Catherine grabs my wrist and yanks it close to her, slapping one of the cuffs around it. The metal is cold and digs into my skin when she snaps it tight. She takes the other cuff and links it to the bedpost.

"Now try to get out of here." She smirks and starts backing away from the bed.

"Catherine, why are you doing this to me?" Tears form rivers down my cheeks.

She stands in the doorframe, her eyes hollow and soulless. "Bad behavior cannot go unpunished. The sooner you learn that, Jess, the better things will go for you."

She steps into the hallway. The door slams, and I hear the lock click. I'm alone and helpless yet again.

CHAPTER TWENTY-TWO

I take the plate with the sandwich in my free hand and huck it as hard as I can at the wall to my left, my chest is heaving with the effort. It smashes into tiny pieces. A thunderstorm roils inside me, rage boiling to the surface.

The lettuce falls limply to the floor. Deli meat slides down the wallpaper, leaving a smear of mayonnaise. The bread splats to the floorboard, stuck there.

If I could reach them, I could use a sliver of broken plate as a weapon. I stay still for a moment, waiting to see if Catherine will burst into the room. There's no sound of her in the hallway, no shadow of her feet in the slit beneath the door.

I lay back on the pillow, panting and sweating, my body a burning furnace. My blood is molten lava. A primal, guttural scream erupts from deep within my chest, from my soul. Reaching as far as I can, I lean down toward the floor, my fingers groping for a shard of broken plate. But every single one has skittered away from the bed. Then I thrash against the bed, against my restraints, frustration erupting from me like the lava in my blood.

Once I've exhausted myself, I flop back against the pillow and wait.

Silence surrounds me.

Has she left the house?

Now I sit and concentrate, regulating my breathing and trying to ease the lightheadedness making me dizzy every time I sit up. I take a deep breath in through my nose and blow it out slowly through my lips. My pulse isn't hammering as violently in my chest anymore. This is a good sign.

If only Catherine lived in a normal neighborhood where the houses were closer together and not spaced out over acres and acres of land. If only her mansion weren't so secluded up the road, tucked too far away from the main highway, I might be able to hear cars going by. I listen anyway, but I'm not sure what I would do even if I *did* hear someone.

Staring at the cuff around my wrist, I decide to take action. No one is getting me out of here. Catherine is too unhinged to let me go, and Mark is on the other side of the world. I'm the one who has to do something about this.

Grunting and gritting my teeth, I grab the handcuff with my free hand, bend my thumb and fingers in as far as I can, and start pulling. The metal sides dig into my skin, leaving red tracks.

I stop to catch my breath for a moment, laying my head back on the pillow. After counting to sixty inside my head, I try again. I've heard of people breaking their thumbs on purpose or deliberately dislocating fingers and joints to get out of handcuffs. *Do I have that kind of superhuman strength?*

I scream again as I push the cuffs down as far as I can, looking in horror at the cuts they're leaving on my skin. The sensitive flesh of my thumb and little finger tears, and the skin becomes red and blistered with fresh blood.

Then I gag. Another wave of dizziness passes over me, and

I'm forced to stop. If I keep going, I'll pass out. Gently, I place my hurt hand back down on the bed and check that my thumb isn't broken. It's not. It's just cut.

Sun floods in through the window, warming my skin. It's pleasant for a moment. I'm so tired. Maybe I should give in and just let her have what she wants, a placid, good little daughter-in-law.

My eyelids are heavy. I blink, but after a few minutes, they fuse shut. Maybe when I wake, I'll be stronger, of more sound mind to make a plan to get out of here. I still have no idea what Catherine's agenda with me is, if she even has one, but I'm not going down without a fight.

* * *

I'm stirred awake by a rustling sound at the door. My eyes bolt open, and my spine snaps up like an arrow. Taking a deep breath, I stare at the door. I don't know how much time has passed. There's no clock, but the light is now a diffused grayish lavender.

I hold my breath as the door creaks open. Catherine enters. The gun is in her hand, by her side. She struts to my side of the bed, but she pauses in front of the mess I've made with the plate and sandwich.

She clucks her tongue, shakes her head, and gives me a disgusted frown as she points at the heap of sandwich on the floor and all the broken plate pieces.

"*This* is how you repay me for making you food?"

I glare at her, saying nothing.

"Suit yourself." She shrugs so casually it makes my blood boil. "I don't have to feed you. I was just trying to be nice. If you want to starve yourself, that's your problem."

"You can't keep me locked away in here forever," I say.

"Who said anything about forever?" Catherine is bent at the knees, picking up the pieces of broken plate and sandwich, taking away my one opportunity for a weapon, if I had ever found a way to reach the broken shards.

Her words send a chill down my spine. "Then what is your plan?"

Catherine sighs as if she's had a trying day and she's exhausted by my line of questioning. "You don't need to worry about it."

"I *do* need to worry about it. You have me handcuffed to a bed. I don't understand what changed, Catherine. Why did you go from doting on me and caring for me to pointing a gun at my face and locking me in here? Is it because I demanded to go to the hospital? That doesn't seem like a triggering enough reason for you to fly off the handle like this."

Catherine chuckles. "You are pushing your luck."

I sink into the pillows, watching her as she tidies up the mess and sets it by the door. She spins on a heel, glowering at me. "You ruined a perfectly good plate and wasted food."

I bite my tongue to keep from arguing with her, just in case she decides to wave that gun in my face again.

She approaches my bed and stands in front of it as if debating whether to sit down next to me, but she remains just out of arm's length.

Tilting her head, she studies me. Her dark eyes have turned almost coal black in the dusky light. I don't understand this change in her. She put on a good show in the beginning and had me fooled for a while, and Mark—well, his entire life has been a lie, and he still has no clue. Catherine is sitting on a throne, the keeper of a kingdom of secrets.

"It didn't have to be this way," she says with sorrow in her voice that sounds robotic.

"Like what? I still don't understand what I did to deserve this." I'm coaxing her, but she's not taking my bait.

Catherine sighs again.

I try one more time. "Catherine, we can fix this. We can go back to how we were."

"No, we cannot." She avoids my eyes.

"Just tell me what I need to do to make you not upset," I plead.

Catherine purses her lips into a tight line and inhales a deep breath then waits a beat before exhaling slowly. Her dark eyes make me shudder. "Just stop talking, Jessica. You know perfectly well what you did." She stands there like a stiff board, her dark eyes trained on me.

"Mark will start to worry if he doesn't hear from me," I point out.

Catherine barks out a laugh. "Hardly. He's across the world. Neither one of us is even on his radar right now."

"That's not true," I tell her. "We FaceTime often. If I don't answer his calls, if he doesn't see my face, he'll think something's wrong."

Something *is* wrong. *Very* wrong.

Catherine chews on her perfectly rouged cherry-red lip.

For a moment, she stares at me, a contemplative expression on her face. I cling to the hope that she's going to let me go, say this was all a misunderstanding, and give me another chance—or at the very least, give me my phone.

If she second-guesses herself, it's short lived. She shakes her head and pounces so fast I don't have time to react.

Catherine grabs my hand before I have a chance to jerk it away, while I'm still stunned. She takes the dangling handcuff and snaps it around my other wrist then bolts it to the bedpost.

My arms are suspended in an uncomfortable, awkward way above my head.

"Catherine, please," I croak, sniffling. "This hurts."

"You don't even know what hurt is, stupid girl." She's snarling through clenched teeth, tightening the new cuff.

"I won't ask questions anymore. I'll behave. Just please, let me have one free hand."

"You don't deserve it," Catherine declares with such finality and disgust that I start to believe that this is it. This is my end. She'll never let me go.

"Catherine, Mark will worry—"

"Shut up!" Catherine draws back a hand and brings it down on my cheek.

The sting is delayed, but when it hits, it roars across my face. I cry out in pain, razor blades shooting across my cheek.

"Stop talking back! Stop talking out of turn! Stop demanding things!" Catherine yells.

I stare at her, my mouth gaping open and my eyes wide with shock.

"You listen to me, and you listen good." She leans in so close to me I can feel her breath on the cheek she just slapped. I want to bring my knees up and slam them into the side of her jaw, but I stop myself because in the end, she's the one with the gun. "You need to start behaving. If you don't, I'll kill you, get rid of your body, and tell Mark you left him. No one will be the wiser."

The blood drains from my face. My heart beats against my ribcage. "You wouldn't do that. I know you wouldn't."

Catherine's pinched lips curl into a sinister smile. "Try me," she says as breezily as if we were having a normal conversation.

She straightens, her eyes pooling with tears, her bottom

lip trembling, and her chin quivering. She starts moving her hands animatedly, waving the gun in an alarming fashion.

"Mark, honey, I'm so sorry," she says. "She just said she couldn't do it anymore. She said she hated me and didn't want to spend one more second in this haunted house with me. Jess told me that the house gave her the creeps, and she didn't love you anymore for leaving her here while you traipsed off to Japan. It's okay, though, honey. I'll take care of you. I'll help you rebuild. You don't need that awful woman who didn't appreciate you, who didn't appreciate *us*. I tried to take her under my wing and help her, but it was no use. Jess is a free spirit. She can't be held down to a traditional lifestyle."

I stare at her in disbelief at this act she's put on so well, crying on cue and everything. She sounds so believable that it's horrifying. If she were to present this to Mark, he would one hundred percent believe her.

Catherine ends her performance with a smirk and a bow.

"Don't underestimate me, you foolish girl." The ice in her voice returns, and her glare is equally as glacial.

She backs away from the bed and marches to the door, picking up the broken plate and ruined sandwich.

"I'll be back in a minute for a punishment for this." She points at the plate. "In the meantime, just sit there and think about what you did." Her laughter is feral. "It's not like you have anywhere else to go."

She slams the door and locks it, for good measure against what, I have no idea. She's right. I can't escape, chained up like this.

I start screaming again, running myself and my voice raw and ragged. Catherine returns several minutes later with a glass of water.

She stands in front of the bed, anger fused into the bones of her face. "We've got to do something about your little screaming fits too. I don't know how you have any voice left after all that carrying on you've been doing."

She takes her thumb and forefinger and lifts my chin. "Open your mouth," she commands, pushing my lips apart. I whip my head back and forth, pinching my lips closed, but I can't fight her off easily with no hands.

"The more you fight it, the worse it will be," Catherine says, trying again, wrenching open my mouth. She manages to get one pill into my mouth, but I spit it out, and it disappears into the sheets.

Catherine roars in frustration, fishing the pill from the tangle of bed linens, and tries to push my clenched jaw open.

"I'll bite you," I warn her.

"If you bite me, you die," Catherine says as if that's the end and she'll accept it for what it is. "Now, open up."

I hesitate, wanting to call her bluff, but I can't risk it. I unspool my tongue, and Catherine sets two pills down on it, the same small capsules she tried to give me the first time I refused.

"Drink these down like a good girl."

She tilts my head back and pours the water into my mouth. I'm so thirsty I gulp it down, powerless to stop it.

CHAPTER TWENTY-THREE

The back of my head throbs dully, and I feel even worse than I did before I went to sleep. My tongue feels too big for my mouth, and my throat is itchy, like there's wool stuck in it. My eyelids are heavy, but I manage to pry them open to find that I'm completely enveloped in darkness.

Panic rises from my gut and spreads through my limbs. The only sound is my sharp, fast breathing.

"Hel—hello?" I call out in an uncertain, raspy voice. "Catherine? Where am I?"

I reach up and wipe the sweat from my face, realizing I'm no longer handcuffed to the bed or even in my room. As I swallow hard, my pulse beats through my eardrums, adrenaline shooting fireworks off inside me. My eyes are not adjusting to the pitch black.

The room smells musty and mildewy, and the air feels wet and a little humid. I fumble around me, trying to grasp for anything I can. Maybe I can find a light switch. My hands scurry across a wall as I rise to my knees, a mattress yielding under my weight. So I'm on a bed, but it's not the *same* bed I went to sleep in.

I can't calm my breathing. Claustrophobia settles over my bones, escalating my panic. My eardrums are ringing, my heart galloping like a wild horse.

"Catherine!" I scream. But something gives me the sense that no one can hear me.

Slowly, I stretch out my arms and feel a stone wall. Then I swing my legs over the side of the bed and find purchase on the floor beneath me. I stand, waiting a moment for the dizziness and nausea to pass. Then I stay rooted to the spot, listening. All I can hear is my frantic breathing.

Once I've calmed, I start padding around with my arms stretched out in front of me, bracing to bump into something. One thing I know is that this is not my bedroom upstairs. I'm in a whole other place. My body is also sore. I check myself over, feeling bruises on the backs of my legs and a lump on the back of my head. *Has Catherine dragged me somewhere?* At least the boot is still on. I can walk relatively well.

My fingers are like antennae fanned out in front of me. In a few steps, my palms hit another wall. I brush my hands over it, hoping for a light switch.

For a few minutes, I flounder in the darkness, my breathing hollow through my eardrums. There are no signs of life besides me. I notice a film of moisture on the wall, but it's not cold to the touch.

I rake my nails across every surface, stretching my arms up, then finally, I hit pay dirt. I fumble with a light switch then flick it upward. The room becomes bathed with dingy yellow light.

Blinking, I wait for my eyes to adjust to the sudden change in brightness. I stand against the wall, backed into a corner, every muscle in my body bracing for a fight. My shoulder blades dig into the concrete behind me.

In the opposite corner sits a twin bed with a flower-print

duvet and a single pillow with a white pillowcase. The bed isn't made, and the imprint of my body is still on the mattress and on the pillow. I shudder, thinking about being asleep down here, unaware of what was going on or how I got here. The bed frame is gold brass and dated.

Near the bed, on the same wall several feet away, a single toilet sits in the corner. It's hooked up to plumbing, but there are no walls or doors around to enclose it. I approach it, inspecting around it. It's clean, and there is water in the bowl. I hit the flusher, and the water suctions out.

Confusion burrows deeper into my brain. There is a small kitchenette on the other side of the room, equipped with a small L-shaped countertop. At the jutting-out part are two plastic chairs, like garden chairs. The cabinets are straw colored, and a white countertop looks like it stepped straight out of a 1970s catalogue. A small white refrigerator sits next to the cabinets.

I stumble over there and start flinging the cabinet doors open. Inside are bags of chips and cookies along with a row of microwaveable sachets of rice.

Then I scramble to the fridge and wrench it open. The fridge light immediately floods the shelves, revealing bottles of water, a gallon of milk, and several casserole dishes covered with aluminum foil.

I peel back some of the foil on one of the dishes. The first one is some sort of chicken concoction. The other has roast beef, carrots, and potatoes. Spaghetti is in the third. *Why is there so much food in here?*

Stepping back, I bump into the countertop then spin around, frightened, jittery, and expecting the worst at any moment.

A note on lined stationary paper I didn't notice before lies on the counter. The paper has an illustration of a robin perched on a tree limb. It's so bright and casual, the kind of stationery a child might use.

I read Catherine's perfect cursive handwriting. With each sentence, things get worse, and I cannot believe what I'm reading.

> *Dearest Jess—*
>
> *I'm sorry things didn't work out. I wanted so badly to take you in as my daughter. I know Mark would have wanted it that way too. He will be so disappointed, I'm sure, but alas, life doesn't always work out the way we want it to.*
>
> *You might as well get used to life down here. These are going to be your surroundings from now on. As you might have already discovered, I left you plenty of food. Don't let it go to waste. I worked hard on the casseroles.*
>
> *—Catherine*

She used the words "down here." I glance up at the ceiling, which is made of wooden paneling, and blow out a deep breath. I must be locked in another part of the basement or something.

I hurry to the door, but it's locked, as I expected. I contemplate screaming again, but I don't know how fruitful those efforts will be.

When I kick the door with my good foot, nothing happens. It doesn't even budge.

"Catherine?" I shout, my mouth pressed near the door. "Are you out there?" I pause a beat but hear nothing but silence. "You'd better answer me!" Still nothing—no movement, no scurrying. There is no slit under the door for me to peer down at to see shadows or movement either.

"Why the hell are you doing this to me?" I pound my fists against the door until I'm exhausted.

Then I limp back to the bed and sit on the edge, listening to the mattress springs groaning in protest.

Cupping my head in my hands, I sob. *What the hell am I supposed to do now?* There are no windows, no way out. I walk over to the drawers and open them. All I find are some old crayons and blank sheets of paper. The locked door. The food. The water. A terrifying thought sinks into my brain. *She might not ever let me out of here.*

CHAPTER TWENTY-FOUR

I don't know how long I sit, as stiff as a board, on the edge of the bed, but it seems to last a long while, like time is stretching its long arms across eternity. Staring at the floor, I keep my hands tucked under my thighs, panting hard, my brain calculating, festering, spiraling.

As icy-hot anger splinters inside me, I glare at the door. This room, with its bed and toilet and tiny kitchenette, has been here for some time, which means that I am not the first person to wake up here. *What happened to the person who came before me? Or people. Plural.*

I've read true-crime accounts of young women—sometimes children—captured and held hostage by creepy men, sometimes for years. I remember one teenage girl giving birth inside a hellhole like this. But that's the thing. I've only ever read about men doing this, not women, which makes me wonder if it wasn't Catherine who built this but Nicholas Hawley, Mark's dad.

Clearly, Catherine knows all about it. Perhaps she knew about it while Nicholas was alive too. I shiver, thinking about Catherine turning a blind eye to Nicholas's sex slave kept locked up in the basement. The thought makes my stomach turn over in disgust.

Then I wonder... *What if Mark knew?*

No, I think. *Surely not.* His father died when Mark was young. It must have stopped afterward. But I can't be certain. I'm making assumptions. Catherine could be the one trapping victims in this moldy room.

I knew as soon as I came to this house that it was as creepy as fuck, from the shadows in the attic to Mark's tale of a ghost.

Wait. What if Mark was telling the truth that night? What if he didn't see a ghost but an escapee from the basement?

I get back on my feet. I will not die here. I refuse to be the latest victim. Catherine may be strong for her age, but she's still over sixty. And she's so unhinged that she surely can't be thinking clearly, or at least, not in the long term. She's bound to make a mistake at some point or another. When she does, I'll be ready.

Though I scan the room for cameras, there's nothing visible in any of the corners. Adrenaline pumps through my veins, and I find myself pacing around the small space, desperately seeking an outlet for all the nervous energy.

The door catches my attention again, and I head over to examine it properly. It's wooden. That's good. Wood is breakable. It's obviously locked from the outside with some sort of key. The lock seems to be fairly normal, though I've already established that I have no idea what I'm doing when it comes to picking locks. There are no windows and no natural light.

Rather than dwell on the present, I go back to my first impressions of Catherine, trying to dissect her behavior and see what I missed the first time around. She was so overly hospitable and seemed too enthusiastic, too chipper in a house filled with shadows and drafts. Catherine was kind, inviting us into her home so we could save for a down payment on a house. It all seemed to align in our favor in the beginning.

I analyze my relationship with Mark, assessing it for anywhere it might have gone wrong, but I can't think of anything. Mark was charming. He had me hooked from the minute I met him. He has always been open and honest with me, always been energetic, adventurous, and he can't be tied down to anything. I know he jumped at the chance to go to Japan, and part of me can't even blame him for that. But he was the one who was raised by Catherine. *How could he not have ever known or been exposed to her madness before? How could he really leave me with her? How could he have been so blind?*

I start to resent him, even though I know he's not my main problem right now. Maybe that's the whole point. Perhaps Catherine wants to build a wedge between Mark and me that becomes so deep there's no recovering from it. Then she'll have gotten what she wants—won, in a sense.

Returning to the edge of the bed, I crumple into the sheets like a piece of paper. It all seems so hopeless. I can allow myself to wallow for a little while. I think about how I gave Catherine more chances than she deserved because I was desperate to have a mother figure after losing my own so young. One I could attach myself to and learn from.

I'd been excited to spend time with Catherine in a big house with a big garden. But Catherine was a hammer, and I was glass. She had shattered all the trust between us to bits. Maybe I'd started it by snooping through her personal boxes in the basement, but she should have found a better way to confront me about it than locking me up.

I'm angry with her for being so cruel, and I'm angry with myself for taking the investigation into her to the next level, for being so naïve as to trust her in the first place, and for giving her loopholes to abuse me. I'm angry with Mark for putting his career before me, even if it feels selfish to say it, and leaving me here with a wicked woman. And I'm angry with him for being so blind to it all, never seeing the warning signs, not for his entire life.

When I unlock the vault of my earliest memories with him, I realize a little too late that six months is not enough time to get to know someone enough to marry them, not if you don't want to deal with the consequences of unearthed secrets. Secrets ruin lives, and I'm neck-deep into someone's secrets that I didn't even realize were possible.

Get up, Jess. Fuck this. Stop wallowing.

I go to the fridge and open it, peruse inside, then pluck out a water bottle. It's sealed, so I know Catherine couldn't possibly have drugged it. I crack open the twist top and guzzle down a few gulps, panting, then wipe away the residue with the back of my hand.

My stomach growls with hunger just looking at the pasta dish, but I can't relent, not yet. I'm not to that breaking point. I have no idea what Catherine might have laced it with to hurt me, knock me out, or maybe even kill me.

I push myself onto the bed, lift myself onto the tiptoes of my good foot, and crane my neck to look into the air vent. I don't see any cameras there, either, no lights blinking that would give away an electronic device.

"Catherine?" I scream into the slits of the vent. "How long are you going to keep me locked in here?"

No answer comes, not that I was expecting one.

"You're crazy!" I yell again, beating the wall with my fists until my hands are bruised and aching again.

I drop down to the bed. If Catherine wanted to kill me, she could have done it when I was passed out from whatever drug concoction she gave me. That's one thing I have going for me.

Also, Mark will miss my FaceTimes. He knows me well enough to know I wouldn't just leave without talking to him. *Doesn't he?* I like to think so. Yeah, we're honeymooners, but it's not just lust with us. We talk things out. But on the other hand, he loves his mother so much that I can see him being pulled into her lies and manipulations.

Fuck. Let's face it—I can't rely on Mark to get me out of here. *Why would his mind even lead him to the basement? Unless he knows.*

I notice something on the wall at the edge of the bed. Frowning, I crawl across the mattress and pull back the covers to get a better look. There are markings on the side of the wall that look like they were colored in with crayon.

Standing, I pull the bed away from the wall, revealing more. These are marks from the poor soul who lived here before me, a person who may or may not be dead now. My skin is cold all over.

I brush my fingertip across the raised ridges in the wood. *Clay.* Someone wrote the name *Clay* over and over again at the baseboards. The name inches upward toward the height of the bed but no further, as if the person writing them wanted to keep them deliberately concealed.

I stumble backward on my heels, staring at the writing.

Then I see words that make my blood run cold.

Help me, Mommy.

The words are in red, like blood.

> Why, Mommy? I'm sorry, Mommy. I won't be a bad boy anymore. Please let me out. Clay. I'm Clay. Clay is a bad boy. Clay must be punished. Mommy is mad at Clay. Mommy is mad. Clay is bad.

I read it over and over, horror tingling down my spine. Tears well in my eyes. I crouch on the floor and stroke the words, salt streaming down my cheeks. I taste it on my lips and lick it away. *How long ago was this written?*

She had a child locked in this room.

The suffering and fright this poor little Clay must have had to live through makes me shake with anger and fear.

"I'm so sorry, Clay," I whisper to his crayon scribbles on the wall. "Who were you? Where are you now, Clay? What happened to you?"

Does his soul haunt this room? What can I learn from him? What other little breadcrumb clues does Clay have hidden around here, just waiting for me to discover them?

CHAPTER TWENTY-FIVE

I DRIFT IN AND OUT OF UNEASY SLEEP. WHEN THE AIR VENT KICKS ON, my eyes bolt open, my breath stilling in my lungs. It takes me a moment to remember where I am. Then it all comes flooding back—Catherine, my broken ankle, her dragging me down here unconscious, the food in the fridge.

She planned it all, but I'm not sure how far back. At least over the last few days, because she needed to cook all this food for me.

I remain still, listening for footsteps or any signs that someone is nearby, either outside the door or in the room, but there's nothing. I don't know whether to feel disappointed or relieved.

During the short fits of sleep, I dreamt about Mark. He was a little boy swimming in the ocean. The water was dark, almost black, so you couldn't see his limbs under the water. He was laughing and playing, his eyes alight with excitement, joy spread across his face.

He was waving to someone or something, then suddenly, his eyes bulged with panic, and he started flailing his arms. I was watching from the beach, but I couldn't do anything to

THE MOTHER-IN-LAW

help him. Then I was hovering over him in the sky. I couldn't see any part of my own body. Mark struggled against the current before being sucked under the water. I waited, a scream stifled in my throat. He didn't resurface.

I woke with tears in my eyes and sweat covering my skin. I slept in the same pajamas I was wearing before Catherine dragged me down here.

Now, I think back to the dream and understand how helpless I felt. Except I'm the one drowning, not my husband. *And what am I going to do about it?*

I have no idea what time it is, whether it's morning, night, or somewhere in between. My stomach grumbles in hunger, and at this point, I know I need to eat. There's no way I can build up enough strength to get out of here without food. Surely, they can't all be drugged. *How long does medication last inside a casserole anyway?*

I open the refrigerator, and my mouth salivates when I peel back the aluminum foil on the chicken dish. There's an expiration date written in black marker in Catherine's handwriting on the foil. I lick my lips. Even unheated, it smells so good, and my starving stomach contracts on cue, desperate for me to stuff my face with it.

Sighing, I lift the casserole dish off the shelf and take it to the counter, peel back the foil, and search the drawers, but there are no utensils, not even a spoon. The only things I can find are paper plates. Clever, Catherine is. She must have learned her lesson not to give me a breakable plate that I can use as a shank.

Taking a deep breath, I gear myself up for what I have to do next. I sink my fingertips into the casserole and scoop out a handful of it, repulsed by the goop but too famished to dwell on it for long.

I plop the food onto the paper plate, set it in the small

microwave sitting on the edge of the counter next to the refrigerator, and lick the residue off my fingers.

On the bright side, if I can even think of one, is at least there is plumbing and electricity down here. But there's no shower, no way to bathe or clean myself. I'm just going to have to make do with the living conditions, if I can even call them that. I have no other choice.

The expiration date on all the food is for about a week from the date I remembered it being when I first woke up down here. Last night, I made a little scratch mark near the bottom of the wood wall where Clay's crayon writings were. That's how I'll keep track of the days, but I have no idea when one will start and the other ends. All I can do is guess or remember to count the hours. I have nothing else to do.

I push the buttons on the microwave. They make a shrill beeping noise against the silence. There's a clock on the front that reads 8:23, but for all I know, it could be the incorrect time. I doubt Catherine bothered to program it before she locked me in here. The microwave hums to life, the plate of chicken casserole spinning around inside it.

When it's finished, I pull it out and immediately dive in to scarf it down, but it's hot, and I burn my tongue, cursing myself for being so desperate.

Once it cools, I scoop in another bite. It's bland, but I choke it down anyway, my stomach grateful to receive sustenance. I wash it down with the same bottle of water I had earlier because I'm trying my best to drink it sparingly in case I really am down here for the long haul.

Once done, I place the foil over the dish again and put it back in the refrigerator, stowing it away for another time.

Afterward, I decide to start doing push-ups and sit-ups along with a few lunges to keep my body limber and agile, to keep my muscles alive and working. I do what I can, pacing myself, choosing exercises that aren't too difficult to manage with the boot on my foot.

Tears spring to my eyes when I think about the boot, what a hindrance it is to me physically, and that I still have to wear it for several more weeks. But that's not what's making me emotional. I might die before my ankle heals.

I don't scream anymore. There's no point. I only use my energy in positive ways, like exercise, meditation, and trying not to lose my mind.

My stomach twists into tight knots when I think about Catherine up there with my phone, with my laptop, with full access to my personal life.

She's probably already gone through all my private messages with Mark, the things we talk about that I would never want to share with anyone, both sexual things as well as fears, hopes, and dreams. Tears flow freely again as I descend into feeling sorry for myself about how unfair the situation is and the cards I've been dealt.

I can't allow myself to think this way for more than a few minutes at a time. Negativity breeds more negativity, and destructive thoughts come with a mental price that I can't afford to pay right now. At least I hadn't told Mark about the letters or meeting with Steven, so there will be no evidence to Catherine that he's involved. I don't want her to hurt him too.

And I can't stop thinking about all the lies she must be feeding Mark. I'm sure she's keeping in touch with him and pretending to be me. She won't want to set off any red flags with him yet. If she weren't worried about it, she would have just killed me already and told him I left him.

There has to be a reason I'm still breathing. I just haven't figured it out yet. *Will Mark be able to notice the subtle differences in the way I punctuate and the way I text to know that it's not me?*

I look down and notice a cabinet underneath the barstools that I didn't see before. It's partially obscured by the stool itself, and the cabinet doesn't actually have a handle. I can see where there might have been one once, but it was long ago broken off. I push the stool out of the way, and it groans across the concrete floor. The sound sets my teeth on edge, so I lift it instead and put it aside.

When I pull on the cabinet front, I'm surprised that it gives way. As it opens, it makes a creaking sound. By now, I'm curious as to why this could be down here in the basement prison. I blow out a slow, deep breath and open the cabinet the rest of the way.

Inside, there's a stack of loose-leaf white papers, which is not what I was expecting. I was hoping for something I could use as a weapon the next time I see Catherine. Nevertheless, I pick them up, prop my back against the wall and stretch my legs out in front of me, setting the stack of papers in my lap.

The corners of the papers are aged, tinged yellow, curling in on themselves. I smooth out the creases with my palm. *Clay* is written in the bottom right-hand corner. I touch his name with my fingertip. Every time I think of this little boy being stuck down here in this prison, my heart breaks.

Carefully, I sort through the papers, analyzing every one of Clay's childish drawings for potential clues. *Who was this child? Why was he here?*

A tear slides down my cheek when I get to one where a little boy is sitting in the corner of the room. He's drawn the bed. His knees are tucked up to his chest, and he's looking downcast. The drawings aren't particularly talented, but there is enough feeling and emotion in them to make me upset when I study them, to know that there were times where he felt alone, scared, and in pain.

Exactly how I feel right now.

There's another drawing where he's created a big bright-yellow sun in the top center of the paper, and the rays are glowing outward. He knew the sun once. He knew the world. Underneath the sun is a boy in motion, a stick-figure drawing. He's wearing blue shorts, a green baseball hat, and his arms are swinging at his sides. There's a huge grin on his face, drawn with thick red crayon for his lips. It's like he's skipping. Clay drew grass under the boy's feet and a tree beside him, with a swing tied on one of the extending branches.

Swallowing a sob, I brush the wetness off my cheeks. This poor boy longed for sunshine and the sensation of grass. I have no idea how much of his life was robbed from him.

I vow to put up a fight or die trying. I will not suffer a fate where I will not ever have the sun warming my shoulders or the breeze tickling my cheeks again. Catherine will not be allowed to take these things from me.

In several of the drawings, in the back is a stick figure of a woman. Clay has colored her to have long hair as yellow as the sun in the other drawing. She has tan skin and brown eyes, identical to Catherine's. I shudder and drop the picture as if it's suddenly caught fire and is burning my skin.

Then I compose myself and lift it again. The woman *has* to be Catherine. She's wearing a pink dress, and her eyebrows are pinched inward in an expression I recognize. She has one stick hand on her hip, and the other one is pointing down. Her mouth is open, with little lines coming out from her lips as if to show that she's scolding.

I quickly put the picture at the bottom of the stack. I can't stomach looking at it another second.

But it helps me begin to put the pieces together.

Clay drew Catherine scolding him, which matches with the messages he left on the wall to his "Mommy." Which means Clay at least thought of Catherine as his mother.

Before Catherine stole Mark from Lily and Steven Roberts, did she steal another child and keep him locked in this basement? But for what purpose? And what happened to Clay?

I glance around the room, my heart pounding, my stomach churning, and my skin slick with clammy sweat. Looking down at my lap, I take several grounding breaths. If I keep gazing around the room, the walls of this already-small space will close in on me.

CHAPTER TWENTY-SIX

As I sort through the rest of the drawings in the stack, I start to notice a trend. In the initial drawing in which I first noticed Catherine, Clay drew her looking angry, her eyebrows arched together as she pointed. I'm starting to realize this was an exception. In most of the other drawings, Clay has given her a sweet smile, fully equipped with red crayon lips that stretch across her whole round face.

Something else I notice about a few of his creations sends icicles traveling up my spine. In some of the drawings stacked at the back, Clay has drawn a man. This man is exceptionally taller than Catherine and Clay, always dressed in a suit with a tie. He's always looming either next to or near Catherine. Not a single drawing shows this mystery man smiling. His eyes are always downcast, a frown always curved into an upside-down U shape on his long face.

In most of the pictures featuring Catherine and this unidentified man, she and the boy, whom I assume to be Clay, are smiling.

Sometimes she's holding Clay's hand. Other times, they're hugging. The man and the little boy never hug, never hold hands, never touch. Neither do the man and Catherine. There is no representation of love between them. I sit back, drinking it in and processing.

Sighing, I rest the back of my head against the wall and gaze at the ceiling. This little boy must have had hours upon hours to draw like this. There was nothing else for him to do, and the depth of that is measured by how many drawings there are. I've lost count.

It was Catherine, Clay, and Catherine's husband, Clay's father. That has to be who this man is. For whatever reason, Clay was locked in this room, but he still loved Catherine. She wasn't horrible to him all the time.

I roll my eyes. *Am I making excuses for Catherine?* No. But I am glad that Clay was shown some kindness.

The relationship between Clay and Catherine must not have all been bad all the time, at least not in the beginning. There must have been a turning point, yes, but Clay wouldn't have drawn these pictures of him holding Catherine's hand or hugging her, both with bright smiles on their faces, if he didn't care for her or feel cared for *by* her—if he didn't have hope.

There's one sizable difference between Clay and me—well, several. For one, I'm not an innocent child. Catherine doesn't love me. She has no reason to save me, nothing to give me to do down here. She doesn't care. At least with Clay, it seems like she tried.

That's beginning to make me wonder whether Clay was Catherine's biological son. It's a reach. I still don't quite understand why Catherine and Nicholas Hawley went around stealing children and one was locked down here in this basement. They gave Mark everything he needed in life. As far as I know, Catherine was nothing but good to my

THE MOTHER-IN-LAW

husband when he was a child, unless Mark has been holding back aspects of his childhood.

I sort through the drawings again, trying to make sense of them and pluck out clues. I see a life in these drawings, which start out rudimentary and slowly become more detailed. The relationship between the child and the "mother" has some loving moments. But I see nothing but fear in regard to Nicholas Hawley. An emotional aching spreads from my heart through my chest, making it feel as if something heavy is being pressed down on it, cracking it into pieces.

Then a memory flashes through my mind, and I cling to it, desperate to filter through every single detail. I start trying to remember what Mark has said about his father. He rarely mentioned him and said he doesn't have very many memories with him.

The memory I have is from right after Mark left for Japan. Catherine and I still had an alliance of sorts, when she still talked to me without everything being veiled and cryptic—back when she still trusted me enough to give me a glimpse into her past.

"My marriage had been filled with many... challenges," she admitted to me over tea on her back terrace one afternoon. I can still see her slender fingers coiled around the base of the ceramic mug.

At the time, I remember sympathizing with her and waiting to hear more about him.

"It wasn't always sunshine and roses." She looked down at her lap with an expression of sorrow and regret. "I... struggled. A lot. He did things that I didn't always agree with, but it was too hard to argue with him, because I didn't want it to turn into an explosive fight. He had a short temper. I walked on eggshells a lot of the time, trying to keep him appeased. It was easier when he was happy. I got to be happy when he was happy. When he was unhappy, my life became very difficult."

She put on such a pitiful performance, and I felt so sorry for her at the time. I was grateful that she had trusted me enough to give me a glimpse into her life with her husband. I even reached across the table and cupped her hand, giving it an endearing squeeze and a delicate smile. "No marriage is perfect. They all take work and compromises."

I felt sorry for her then but not now. There has to be a line. Locking away a small child without trying to do something about it is the line, surely. Locking *me* in this dingy prison cell —that's evil. She has it in her, too, no matter how much she may reframe her marriage and her own nature in her mind.

Then there's Mark's insistence that he saw someone in his bedroom as a child. *A ghost or Clay?* If it *was* Clay, then he found a way to escape. I glance at the drawings, my fingers pressed into the stacks of pages and pages. I'm holding a literal key to the past, a piece of someone else's tortured history. If Clay potentially escaped this room, then maybe I can too.

I set the pile of drawings on the floor and get on my hands and knees, scrounging through the cabinets behind the barstools. Tucked away in the darkness, covered in a layer of dust and cobwebs, are a few toys—stuffed animals. One bear with an eye missing. It looks worn, like at one point it had been loved and cherished.

There is also a little blue bin of crayons. I rummage through the shelves, find a stack of notebooks at the bottom, and lift them out. Flipping to a blank page, I lick my lips. Then I go sit in front of the wall where Clay has drawn things and written words.

Everything that he has written on the wall is a jumbled mess, so I start jotting it all down onto the notebook paper to make sense of it. The messages are short, but they're haunting. Even if they say little, they speak volumes.

> Monday fun day. Tuesday food day. Wednesday no day. Thursday sad day. Friday food day. Saturday happy day. Sunday clay day.
>
> So was that his routine every week, and if so, did it always involve Catherine?

Food day makes my heart hurt. He was waiting for someone to come and feed him. That was all he did that day. Then *no day*. I've never known two words to pierce my soul before, but they do. And at that point, I want to kill Catherine. I want to snap her neck and watch the life drain out of her eyes.

Then I distance myself from the emotion. I need to think through it all clearly.

Sitting back, I tap the crayon against my chin, the notepad resting in my lap. I wonder if he wrote these things on the wall before Catherine relented and gave him paper. Then again, it must have been in an act of desperation or something he didn't want her to find, because the writings on the wall are hidden behind the bed frame.

These sentences mean something. He had a schedule with Catherine. She came to visit him. She would give him attention, except for *no day*, when he received no visits, no food, no nothing. *What could* Clay day *mean?*

Swallowing down the lump in my throat, I listen out for any signs of life. I study every corner of the wall, every crevice, for what seems like the hundredth time, but I have to be diligent. A prickly sensation travels across the back of my neck, like I'm being watched, but I can't find any proof of cameras.

I tuck my knees up to my chest and wrap my arms around my ankles, rocking myself back and forth, a new hobby that I hate because it makes me feel like I'm going crazy.

I know I'm spiraling. I'm descending into this madness, this dark depression, but I'm powerless to stop any of it.

If I can't control my emotions as an adult, I cannot even begin to imagine the fear that little boy had. Or maybe it wasn't as bad for him. Maybe he still had the hope that only a child could cling to, the naivety that only a little boy would have, one who desperately sought approval and love from his parents—no matter how wicked they were. Maybe he saw the good in people and in situations in general.

One question still lingers in my mind. *Why?*

Nothing about these drawings or sketches suggests that Clay was kept down here to be tortured. And yes, I did worry about one thing I hoped wasn't true—*What if Mark's father or even Catherine herself was a pedophile?* The thought makes me want to vomit, but it also makes sense in this context. *Why else would they keep a child locked down here?*

But Clay would have drawn or written something about the abuse. I'm not sure. I wonder if he could even give those moments a voice. I live in hope that he wasn't hurt down here.

Then I have to wonder why one child was kept in the basement while Mark was allowed to live freely. I know that Mark was snatched, but I'm not sure about Clay. Perhaps the kidnapping didn't go as successfully with Clay. Maybe Catherine was concerned someone would find him, so they had to hide him.

I push myself off the wall and go over to the bed to peer up at the air vent. I can't get a good look, so I hobble onto the bed and stand on the mattress. I'm a little wobbly, but I manage to stand on the tiptoes of my foot that's not in the boot. Still, I can't get high enough to see inside the vent. I stretch my arms out, but I can't reach it to pull it down.

I stare into its blackness, wondering what's inside. *Is this how Catherine's watching me if she is watching? Is this the way Clay escaped?* It doesn't add up. If he was a child, he'd be even shorter. There's no way he would be able to crawl his way inside here, and I see it's too narrow of a space now that I'm inspecting it further.

I turn around, frowning, my hands on my hips. Then I climb down from the bed and search the whole room, trying to peel apart the parts of the floor and walls that have wood paneling, but it's no use. I work until my fingernails are chipped and my knees and the pads of my fingers are scratched and bruised.

After I'm done, I sit in the center of the room, breathing hard and brushing my shaking fingers through my hair.

It hits me like a freight train. *I am going to die here.*

My breaths are cold, constricted in my throat. *No. That isn't an option. I can't die here.*

Clay died in here.

No, I don't know that for sure.

But where is he if he didn't die down here? Did they punish him for trying to escape?

A panic attack is building up from my chest. I try to push it down. Sour sweat erupts from my pores. I haven't had a shower in days. I wash in the sink as best as I can, but I must smell terrible. And now the fear is coming out of me.

There is a chance that I might die a long, agonizing death in this place. *If Catherine never comes back for me...*

No. I won't allow myself to think that. She will come down here. And when she does, it's me or her, and I choose me. I will get out of here no matter what. Then I'll tell Mark exactly who this woman is and how evil she is. I picture her in handcuffs, being led away by the police. Then I picture myself finding a weapon. A knife. Something heavy. A hammer. I picture her lying on the ground, covered in blood.

I push the heels of my palms into my eyes and rub them across my face. My heart rate kicks up, like hummingbird wings flapping, and searing panic continues to surge. My stomach is a thunderstorm, and tears pool in my eyes.

Perhaps Catherine is up there right now, thinking about ways to kill me. She could slip down here when I'm asleep and place a pillow over my face. Or she could bring her gun into this room to shoot me in the head.

Maybe she won't need to kill me. I'm going so crazy I'll do it myself. I don't know how. *Bedsheets around my neck.*

I get up and move around. No. I won't go crazy. Thinking about killing that bitch is what's going to keep me alive. I get down on the ground, ignoring the boot and the stench coming up from the cast around my ankle. There's no pain anymore. Maybe my boot will end up being a weapon.

I exercise, doing as many sit-ups as I can followed by squats and push-ups. I will be strong. I will be ready. If she wanted to kill me, I'd already be dead.

But I know for certain—I want her dead, and I want to see her suffer.

CHAPTER TWENTY-SEVEN

I'M DEVELOPING A ROUTINE IN THIS HELL. I SLEEP TO PASS THE TIME. When I can't sleep anymore, when I need to release the tension and the volcanic level of energy, when I need to be visceral, I exercise. I prepare for the moment Catherine walks through that door.

I walk, pacing. I do push-ups, crunches, and arm exercises. As best as I can, I do lunges to keep my leg muscles working. Existing in this cave with no music, no books, and no one else to pass the time with is making my brain feel foggy, making me feel disconnected from reality. If I don't stay active, I'll become a zombie.

Because I crave structure, I time everything out perfectly. Rather than gobble down the food Catherine left, I wait until the last possible second, when my stomach is twisted into knots of hunger, before I eat. I wait to drink until my throat is as dry and gritty as the Sahara Desert.

I want to stay strong to keep my energy levels going, but I have to be smart and ration my supplies. If I drain my food and drink, I'll have nothing left.

Something in my gut tells me that Catherine will be back

to replenish the supplies, but I don't know when that will be. It could be in a week. It could be tomorrow. But I'll be ready to fight for my life. I've trained my body, even in sleep, to be aware, always listening out for threats. I've always been a light sleeper, something that used to bother me, but now it might save my life. Still, fatigue, boredom, and the lack of natural light are taking a toll on my mental and physical state, even if I'm trying to deter it.

I try not to focus on the misery, but there are times when I sob. Sometimes, I'm able to successfully trick my brain into thinking that I'm just in an office, that this is temporary, or that I'm in a hotel room. I pretend that this is my apartment and I've just come home from a long day at work. I exercise then make a plate of food, sit, and eat as if I'm a single person living on my own. Sometimes, it works. Other times, it doesn't.

When it doesn't, I sleep. When I can't take it anymore, I resort to screaming again.

Eat.

Sleep.

Exercise.

Scream.

Repeat.

Make the bed. Stretch. Meditate. Eat when I'm hungry. Meditate when I'm at a breaking point.

I pace a lot.

I count in my head—my footsteps, the workout steps, the number of times I chew then the number of swallows I take, the number of times I go to the bathroom. I count the days, marking them on the wall near Clay's writings.

One time, after a particularly restless sleep, I wake up in a cold sweat from a nightmare in which Catherine came into my room with a chainsaw and started hacking through my leg right where my boot begins.

The blankets tangled around me are damp. Adrenaline pumps through my veins. I fumble my hands over my legs and breathe out a sigh of relief when they're both still attached. It was only a dream. The soggy sheets are full of sweat, not blood.

I crawl up to a standing position and beat my fists against the walls, screaming into the air vents. I have no idea what time it is, but I yell anyway. It's silent all the time.

I get a slice of satisfaction in hoping that Catherine can hear me and that I'm making her just as crazy as I feel. I want her to suffer like I'm suffering.

My pounding motions reverberate through my bones, shaking them and the walls.

Even though it exhausts me, screaming is one of the few outlets I have, where I can experience some form of retaliation at Catherine's expense.

I make the noise, the wails, the banging, reminding Catherine that I'm down here. I haven't shriveled into a ball and given up. She hasn't broken my spirit yet. She hasn't killed me. I will not be forgotten, abandoned, discarded like a piece of trash.

When my boredom gets out of control but I'm too tired to fight the walls and the air vents, I sort through the cabinets again and examine the contents of each shelf meticulously. They're deep, and it's taking me a while to get through them all. Toward the back, there are toys. I take them out and inspect them.

I run my fingers along the top of a toy truck, tears flooding my eyes. These toys have been forgotten. Most of them are stuffed toys. I search for something, anything, I could break to create a sharp point—a weapon. But there's nothing.

Instead, I look for clues hidden within this pile of toys. Some of them are more worn than others, especially the small stuffed animals. I imagine Clay using these toys as friends, lining them up as comfort, as a form of security. There's a picture in my mind of what Clay looked like. I keep making him resemble my husband when he was a child, but that's silly. As far as I know, Clay and Mark weren't related. Mark is Lily and Steven's child.

I find a stack of notebooks in the back, covered in a layer of dust, forgotten over the years. I'm about to reach for them when I hear something. I freeze with my heart stilled momentarily.

It could just be my mind playing tricks on me. It's happened before but is starting to become more frequent. I'm learning that the brain will create sounds if it's suspended in silence for too long. But even if it always ends up being just my imagination, I can't afford to ignore it.

Pushing myself off the floor, I listen to the vibration in my ears, my muscles flexed like bricks. The only sound is the pounding of my pulse through my eardrums.

I take a few careful steps toward the door, but there is no slit to look under. Then I press my ear to the door, straining my ears to hear movement.

But I hear nothing. Yet I could have *sworn* I heard something before. It sounded like someone dropped something, something like metal clanging against a concrete floor.

I stand there with my ear against the door for about a minute, maybe longer. Then I turn my body and listen with the other ear just in case. I wait another full minute, ticking the seconds off inside my head. There's no more noise.

I go to the air vent and yell into it. "Catherine, is that you?

Were you outside my room? Can you hear me? I know you can hear me." I don't know it for sure, but I want to make her nervous, make her sweat if she can hear me.

For several minutes, I obsess over the noise, but when nothing else happens, I retreat for now and curl back up in the corner with the notebooks.

The first one begins with drawings, like the ones he's drawn before. He always signs his name at the bottom. They must be from a more recent stack, because I can tell a difference in the quality. It hits me then that I have seen Clay's progression in drawing ability, which means he may have been in this room for years.

I push the thought away before it consumes me and immerse myself in the notebooks. Then I flip to a page with something different. The drawings stop here and become replaced with thoughts, notes, emotions scribbled on a page.

These are Clay's diary entries. His deepest, darkest, most private thoughts are loaded on the pages, just waiting to be found. And I'm going to devour them, every last word, hunting out answers like a rabid animal.

CHAPTER TWENTY-EIGHT

Clay uses crayon in big, boxy handwriting that takes up more than one line in the pages. He writes like a child who has just learned to write well and is trying his best to be good at it and make a good impression. The diary begins almost optimistic, like he thinks it's a game to be trapped down here. But I steel myself, knowing that these words are going to be incredibly sad.

On the other hand, I can't believe my luck that Catherine left these journals down here. It has to be a mistake, something she overlooked. I find it hard to believe that she would deliberately leave all these for me to find. These diaries may explain how Clay escaped that day. That's the part I need to find.

So I dive in.

There are no dates, but Clay writes his age at the top of each entry. He also writes each entry in a different color, which helps distinguish them. I swallow down my angst and begin reading each line.

> I'm Clay, I'm 6.
> Today was a good day. Mommy let me watch TV. Mommy says when I'm a good boy, good things happen. I try to be a good boy every day, but she still tells me I can't come out of this room. I don't get it. When I ask her why, Mommy gets upset and says it has to be this way.

I take a deep breath and keep reading, realizing my fingers are shaking the pages. I ball them into fists and steady my breathing. Some of the words are spelled wrong or written phonetically, like he was trying to sound them out when he wrote each letter. It's heartbreaking to see.

> I'm Clay, I'm 7
> Mommy came to see me today. She looked tired. We watched a movie with fish in it. Mommy didn't want to play. She closed her eyes and rubbed her head. When I asked her what was wrong, she told me she had a bad day. I asked her if it was because I was bad, and she said no, of course not, and started stroking my cheek. That made me feel a little better. I snuggled on her lap while I watched the movie. Mommy brushed her fingers through my hair. I love it when she does that.

I'm Clay, I'm 7

Mommy didn't come today. I must be a bad boy. I cried today. I'm glad no one saw. I wish there was a window in this room. I want to see the outside. I want to play outside. I know there is an outside. Mommy said the house is real big. I want to run up and down the stairs and down the hallways. I dream about it. I want to jump and run a lot. Sometimes I jump and run in this room, but it's not very big.

I'm Clay, I'm 7

Mommy came to eat dinner with me today. We had hot dogs and chips. She even let me have juice instead of water. I asked her if I could have soda, but she said no. I was still happy to spend time with her. She seemed happy today. I could tell it by her eyes and her smile. When she left, I got sad and cried. I asked her if I could come with her, and she said it wasn't a good idea.

I'm Clay, I'm 7

This entry is different. It is where his words start to get dark and frustrated. He writes this one and several others after it in red, with large letters and lots of underlining. I am in awe of what he can do, how he can write so well at only seven years old. Maybe he was on the verge of being eight. I start to wonder who taught him to write. He doesn't mention anything in the entries about being homeschooled.

Mommy says I have a brother. His name is Mark. She showed me pictures of him. She won't let me see him. She said that we would be best friends. I begged Mommy to let me play with him, but she got upset and started crying. I don't like it when Mommy cries. I hugged her and told her I was sorry. I don't want to make Mommy mad anymore. I will be a good boy from now on. I will dream about playing with Mark. I wonder if he likes to jump and run like me.

I pause here for a moment, trying my best to process this information. My stomach is twisting itself into queasy knots of distress. I knead my fingers into the nape of my neck, ironing out the strain from siting in this position so long and the tension from all the emotional stress. I stand up and go to the bed then plop down on it, resting the journals in my lap and propping myself up on a pillow to keep reading, in disbelief.

> My daddy hates me. He doesn't like the way I look. He thinks I'm a freak. Mommy says it's not true, but I think she's lying. If she wasn't lying, then she would let me out of this room. I asked Mommy why Daddy never comes down to visit me. She says it's because he's busy. I asked if he was busy playing with Mark. She shook her head and started to cry again, but she didn't really give me an answer. I don't know what I did wrong.

> I'm Clay, I'm 8. I don't want to live in this room anymore.

The entries are starting to get more desperate, more urgent for answers and for a way out. I swallow hard and stand up, stretching out the kinks in my body and working out the wrinkles in my soul.

I walk to the fridge and open it to pluck out a water. I take a few sips then a few deep breaths. Closing my eyes, I pretend I'm anywhere but here, wondering if Clay used the same methods. I suddenly can't breathe in here.

I'm suffocating in the stale air. I can't push air into my lungs.

The water bottle slips from my fingers and hits the ground. I hear the water leaking out and feel its coldness tickling the edge of my bare foot, but I don't reach for it. I don't bother to pick it up.

Instead, I lean into the counter then slide down the cabinet, my head in my hands. Giant, unrelenting sobs crackle in my chest and explode from my throat. My fingers tangle in my hair, and I press my forehead to my knees.

It takes me several minutes to compose myself, and when I do, my eyes are puffy. I crawl to the bed and place the notebooks aside. I can't look at that torment anymore right now. The isolation Clay experienced is an exact replica of the torture I'm going through right now.

I pull the covers over my head and curl into a ball, lying under the protective cocoon with my arms over my head, as if I'm anticipating a physical blow to come out of nowhere. I wouldn't be surprised at this point. I've taken enough emotional blows for today, so one more won't make a difference. Squeezing my swollen, stinging eyes shut, I lie there until I'm numb, drained of all tears, like a hollowed-out shell of a human. I surrender to sleep, sinking into the darkest crevices of my unconscious.

* * *

I don't know how long I sleep, but my neck and back are sore when I wake up. Rubbing my shoulders, I yawn and stretch, my brain lurching me into a sitting position when I realize I'm still trapped in this damn basement.

I glance to my left. Clay's notebooks are strewn out beside me. I sigh and pick up the same one I was reading from then flip to the current page.

When I glance at the kitchen area, I remember that I dropped my water bottle. The puddle is still sitting there, spreading across the dingy linoleum. I don't care. I leave it there.

I absorb myself back into Clay's entries, rested enough to be able to emotionally take the agony of it all.

> I'm Clay, and I'm sad. I'm also 9 years old.
>
> Today I got really bored, so I tried to escape. There's a hole above my bed. Mommy called it the air vent, and she told me not to touch it. I tried, but I couldn't reach it. I think it's too small. When Mommy came to visit me, as soon as she opened the door, I ran past her before she could close it again.
>
> I just ran and ran. It was dark. There

were lots of hallways. I found stairs and ran up them. Mommy was yelling at me, chasing me. I didn't care. I just kept running. She couldn't catch me. I was too fast for her. That made me happy.

I don't know how far I got. I don't know where I was going. I just wanted to see more and find Mark.

But Daddy found me first. Daddy wasn't happy.

The entry stops abruptly. I gulp and reluctantly flip to the next page with a heart hammering like rain against pavement.

Clay is a bad boy. Daddy is angry. Daddy hurt me. Daddy yelled in my face and told me I was a bad boy. Daddy told me I can't escape again. He kicked me and hit me. I have bruises now. They hurt. Mommy didn't help me. Mommy should have helped me. Mommy is bad too.

I scream and throw the notebook across the room. It smacks the wall and falls to the floor. Heat spreads through me, and I ball my hands into fists and roar before walking over to the wall and picking up the journal.

"I'm sorry, Clay," I whisper, for throwing his words

against the wall and also for what he endured from the hands of his mother and father.

Then I go back through some of the entries I've read. One part sticks out to me. *Daddy says I'm a freak.* I wonder if Clay had some sort of disfigurement. Puzzle pieces begin to fit into place. Catherine's biological son, Freddy, died young of a rare genetic disorder. Clay writes about how his father thinks he looks strange.

Is that why they locked him away?

Jesus.

The thought makes me want to throw up. I didn't think it was possible for my estimation of Catherine and Nicholas to sink any lower, but it has. They are the evilest people I've ever known. I thumb through the pages of Clay's diary. He's a sweet boy who shows love for his mommy even in these circumstances. For the most part, she shows him kindness too.

Yet she didn't go against her husband. She never released Clay.

> I'm Clay, I'm 10.
>
> Mommy brought me a soda and paper to draw on. She says I should draw as much as I can because I'm good at it. Then we watched a movie about a dog that talks, and she showed me more pictures of Mark. I think she loves Mark more than me, but that's okay. Mark doesn't have a funny face like me, so I guess that's why. But it's okay. I still love Mommy.

CHAPTER TWENTY-NINE

Life is passing me by one ticking second at a time, and it's hell. I sit in the corner, cold and starving, my hair a stringy, oily mess curtaining around my face.

What is Mark doing right now? What time is it in Tokyo? I picture him in some posh rooftop bar, clinking shot glasses filled to the brim with sake, some of it sloshing over the rim before he draws it to his parted lips. I picture the strobing lights of Tokyo lighting up his face and hear the rhythm of the traffic in sync with his pulse. I see the nightlife, the high rises, and the restaurants. I smell the fried meats cooking in carts on the street and see their steam rising and dissolving in all the neon and sparkle.

Does he miss me? Does he wonder why I haven't FaceTimed him? I'd love to know what excuses Catherine has thought up. I imagine her crying through the phone, admitting that we had a huge argument and I left. She tells him that I don't care about him and that I don't love him. She whispers poison, manipulating him. I'm sure my phone is full of missed calls. Maybe he's in Japan, worrying about me and considering whether to come home. But Catherine will tell him that I'm fine and he shouldn't bother because I'm a cold-hearted bitch and he can do better.

And what about me? Do I still love my husband? Knowing what I know now about his family?

I need to know if he ever knew about this room. If he did, even when he was a tiny child, I just don't know. *Could I ever look at him the same way?*

I think about my job and what Catherine might have done, if anything, to get them off a suspicion trail. I can picture her sitting with my laptop at her kitchen counter, her glasses low on her nose as she squints at the screen, the gold chain swishing around her neck as she moves her head. She types in some excuse to my boss and my clients about my extended absence. I clench my jaw. She'll make something up that will be believable enough. It's what Catherine does best, of course, tricking people, manipulating them, gaslighting them. Maybe she has even reported me missing. Perhaps the police have been in the house, walking across floorboards above my head. I don't know to what extent Nicholas and Catherine have made this place soundproof.

Putting my head in my hands, I begin to weep. It's all just too much. I'm drowning down here. The world moves on, and I am lost.

* * *

I'm on the floor, doing crunches, using a blanket as padding. I need to burn off some of this steam, my hatred for Catherine, inside me. I don't use that term lightly, either, but I despise her for what she's done to me, to Clay, to Lily, Steven, and even to Mark. She's lied to him his whole life.

Once I get through five hundred crunches, I stand up and start throwing air punches. I close my eyes and pretend I'm landing blows on Catherine's eye socket and on her jaw. I'm pounding my knuckles into the back of her head. It feels good. It helps. I punch and punch until I'm exhausted, my arms burn, and I can't stand up anymore. The room spins, and I grab the edge of the bed and sit, winded.

Running my hand through my hair, I wish I had a shower. I've never wanted to brush my teeth so badly in my life. I graze my tongue across my teeth and gums. It feels like there's fur growing on them. My armpits smell like sour milk.

Despite the stomach-churning stench, I'm hungry—ravenous, in fact. I open the fridge door and stand there for a few extra seconds, allowing the cold air to sink into my hot pores. The casseroles are more than half-gone. The ones that are left are beginning to smell a little funky. My water supply is running low too. A pile of empty plastic bottles sits on the floor in the corner. There's a faucet in the kitchen, but I have no idea if the running water is safe to drink. Soon, I'll find out.

I slam the fridge door shut, and a thunderous scream bellows from my throat with a loud boom that startles me. I stomp my good foot and crane my neck up to the vent, yelling into it. "I'm almost out of food, Catherine! You're going to have to come down here and face me eventually."

As usual, nothing happens. My screams go ignored, and only silence answers me. Maybe Catherine will leave me down here to starve to death, but the more I toss scenarios around in my head, the more I begin to think she doesn't have it in her to kill me or even let nature take its course. Killing me would mean she'd have to dispose of me. It makes things too complicated, and I think she knows it and doesn't want to deal with it. But she's also thinking about how she can't let me go because she's afraid I'll go directly to the police.

Maybe Catherine didn't kill Clay either. She spent time with him down here, watching movies and giving him soda.

She's an evil, evil bitch, but I'm still not sure she's a murderer. Evil can be quiet and insidious. It's allowing your husband to lock away your child. It's stealing someone else's baby from a hospital because you know there's a chance your baby may be born with a genetic disorder. Sadism is Catherine's husband physically assaulting a child and controlling a family with an iron rod.

The question is: Can Catherine murder her daughter-in-law?

I shake my head slightly and groan. I'm so sick of this place, sick of my thoughts and of wondering if I'm going to die today. I'm tired of looking at these four walls. Then I stare down at my boot and wonder for a moment how long I've had it on now. It's been weeks, so it could be almost healed. All I know is that I want it off. I'm hot and sticky and can smell the dirty skin down there.

Sitting on the floor, I lean against the side of the bed and draw my knee up to my chest to start fiddling with the straps of my boot. As I unstrap the sections, I envision myself naked in a shower, the water streaming over my face and rolling down my back. I run my soap hands across my body, scrubbing out the filth and sweat. I imagine myself tipping back a bottle of mouthwash, drinking it straight from the bottle and swishing it around in my mouth, refreshing my gums and teeth and peeling away the grit from my tongue.

I get to the last strap of my boot and unlatch it. It's liberating, like storm clouds parting, like the adrenaline high after you cross the finish line at a race. My foot starts to throb and itch in anticipation. I grip each side of the boot and begin to carefully pull it off, grimacing, expecting pain to pulse through my ankle.

Once the boot is off my foot, I set it aside. My heart thrums. My whole leg feels lighter but also like it's made of gelatin. The first thing I do is rake my nails across my toes. The cast is still there, my skin itching underneath. *Could I get the cast off somehow?*

Still sitting, I set my foot down then push a small amount of weight down on it. My ankle aches dully, but it's not something I can't handle. If I could just get this cast off. But I can't. There's nothing even remotely sharp in this room. But I'm not putting the boot back on. I refuse to be hindered by that heavy, bulky thing one more second.

I pick it up and weigh it in my hands. It's heavy enough that I could use it as a weapon if I need to. I could clock Catherine in the side of the head with it. Maybe it would even knock her out. Now I know I can put weight on my cast, I don't even need to wear it. I smile as I create the image of her eyes rolling back in her head as she tumbles to the ground after I slam the boot into the side of her temple.

"I'll get an opportunity," I murmur. "Revenge will come soon. I can feel it in my bones."

Defiance fuels me. I push myself off the floor and stand there for a moment or two, debating whether to try walking around a bit. I'll need to put motion back in my ankle if I want to have any chance of defending myself against Catherine. Maybe I can try what Clay did and bolt once she does open the door.

The prospect excites me, quickening my pulse. Clay was a defenseless little boy who ran into his father before he could get very far into his escape. Well, his father is dead. There's no one to barricade me if I successfully break out of this godforsaken hole in the ground.

I put a little weight on my injured foot, holding my breath and bracing for pain, but it's more of a noodley sensation. The cast is cumbersome. *But can I run in it?* I put a little more weight on it, testing the waters and giving my ankle time to adjust to the added pressure.

A throb shoots through my ankle and across my foot. I curl my toes in response and suck in a sharp breath, but it's nothing I can't handle. It's not agonizing pain, which is a great sign.

Crutches would be a good way to transition from the boot to regular walking, but I don't have the luxury of crutches. I'm going to have to rehabilitate myself the old-fashioned way and bite through the uncomfortable throb.

I take a deep breath and a simultaneous step forward. Okay. This isn't so bad. I can do this. I can get used to walking. I try not to limp, try not to bear too much weight one way or the other. Eventually, I'll be able to make it even on both sides, and my body will adapt to the use of both feet.

It will just take practice.

It's not like I have anything better to do than count the seconds passing me by. It will give me something better to focus on besides debating my fate.

I pad to one end of the wall and back again, smiling in pride when it gets easier, and my foot stops feeling like it's made of beanbag. My ankle still twitches in pain if I put too much weight on it, but if I keep getting stronger, maybe eventually, I will be able to run.

Run out of here.
Run away.
Run to safety.
Run from Catherine's eternal torture.

CHAPTER THIRTY

I'M GETTING BETTER AT WALKING WITH MY CAST. IT'S STILL A LITTLE cumbersome, but each time I put weight on it to take a step, the sharp ache in my ankle dulls to a throb until it nearly vanishes.

I keep practicing, keep stepping. I count my steps. So far in this session, I'm up to nine hundred twenty-nine. It's a lot for these cramped quarters. I relish the way my heart rate kicks up, my pulse thrumming through my head.

I want to run, to burst from this room like a tornado and never look back, putting a Jess-shaped hole in the drywall.

Tired from all the walking, I pick up Clay's journals and take them over to the bed. I'm pretty sure I've read them all now, but I want to look through them again in case there's something I've missed.

Toward the end of the journals, his entries are shorter.

I didn't get any food today. There is a large space where he didn't draw or write anything else down. At the bottom of the page, he wrote, *Daddy doesn't love me.* Directly under that, he wrote, *Mommy doesn't love me.*

A sob bubbles in my throat, but I swallow it down.

The entry on the next page is a little more uplifting. He sounds happier.

Mommy came today! I was happy to see her. She smiled a lot and hugged me a lot. She even let me watch cartoons and brought me comic books. She told me to read them when I get bored.

Then at the bottom of the page, he wrote, *I get bored a lot.*

I flip to the next page, and a loose sheet of paper tumbles from the back of the book. As I read it, my blood runs cold.

It's too dark.

I hear scary noises.

I keep my eyes closed because I'm afraid of bad things.

Mommy stayed with me until bedtime tonight. I was happy. I asked her to stay with me until I fell asleep, and she said yes! I was glad I wouldn't have to go to sleep alone in the dark this time. Mommy ran her fingers through my hair, and it felt good and made my eyes feel heavy.

There is a blank space before he continues. It's written in green crayon, whereas the first part was written in black, but I'm pretty sure it's the same journal entry.

Mommy even stayed to read me a bedtime story. It was about this boy named Harry. Harry could do magic. He got a letter that told him he was going to go to this special magic school.

Harry lived under the stairs at his house. I liked that part because it made me feel like I'm special too. His room sounded cozy. Maybe mine isn't so bad because it's bigger.

But mine doesn't feel as cozy.

And Harry gets to come out of his room.

I don't.

That makes me sad.

I sat up straight in my bed and started jumping up and down.

Mommy didn't like that. She told me to stop. But I was happy because I said I might get a letter, too, to go to a magic school.

Mommy put her hand on my knee and patted it, but then her eyes got really red. She put her head down and started to cry. I hugged her real close and told her I won't go if she doesn't want me to go to the magic school. But Mommy just cried and cried until I got upset and started crying too.

I told Mommy she shouldn't be sad because she doesn't have to live under the stairs or in the basement. But that just made Mommy cry harder.

Mommy stopped crying, but she was breathing real fast. Her eyes were on me and sort of red. She took my hand and held it too tight. She said if I wanted to get out of here, I should hit her in the left knee.

I asked her why she wanted me to hit

her in the left knee. She licked her lips and took a deep breath. She looked down at her lap. She held my hand too tight still.

She told me she has a bad left knee. If I kick there, she'll fall, and if I get out, Daddy won't be mad at her because he knows she'll be hurt.

But I don't want to hurt Mommy.

I could never hurt Mommy.

I told her I can't do it. She nodded, wiped her eyes, gave me a hug, and tucked me into bed. She told me not to worry and to think about it.

I lay in my bed in the dark, thinking about it.

I don't want to kick Mommy.

But I do want to leave this room.

CHAPTER THIRTY-ONE

My food supply ran out two days ago. I drained the last of the chips and cookies. Not a crumb remains. I even braced myself and ate the old casseroles, despite the smell. One didn't stay in my stomach long, but the rest were fine.

Was it two days ago? I don't even know anymore. I made marks on the skirting board, but I don't know when. The hours blur together because I sleep a lot. When I sleep, I dream about Mark bursting through the door, ready to save me. Or I picture Catherine bleeding out on the ground because I've stabbed her in the heart.

When I'm awake, my stomach contracts from hunger. Bruises cover my hands from pummeling the door. I listen for her footsteps. Sometimes, I imagine them. I stand by the door, waiting.

Then I pace. Then I sleep. I count my breaths. I hold my abdomen in pain. I push the pain down and stand, forcing myself to my feet, ready.

I am ready for her.

Then I'm not, because I think I'm going to die.

I go back to bed and sleep.

When I wake, I sit cross-legged on the cold floor with my ear pressed to the door, straining to hear anything. *Anything.* I'm convinced she's coming for me. I'd give anything just to hear a little sound, any sign of movement, that there is life and living beyond this room.

For a long time, I hear nothing, but I don't give up. When my neck and back get tired of being in that position, when my hips and the bottom of my spine are numb, I get up and move around, then I go back, readjust my body, and angle my other ear to the door.

The prospect of hearing something going on out there is what keeps me going. Hope is a dying flame inside my chest, but every now and then, I give it air, and the flame expands, lighting me up from within. I don't give up. To give up is to succumb to death, and I will not do that, not yet. I need to hang on for a little while longer. I sense a change is coming, like a giant storm brewing on the horizon that hasn't reached the fields yet.

Sighing, I turn around, propping my back against the door. I have the orthopedic boot by my side, ready to smack her with. Sometimes, I even sleep with it next to me. It stinks, but I don't even care anymore. This is my weapon. It is a part of me.

I look at the collection of items I've put into separate piles on the other side of the room next to the wall. Clay's drawings are the first in the row, then his journals, then his toys, and after that are the hardcover books he was given to read.

They are in piles according to possible use, things I can throw at Catherine or hit her with. I even sorted out the crayons, thinking that I might be able to use them to stab Catherine in the eye. Imagining charging at Catherine, plunging that crayon as deep into the socket as I can get it, brings me more pleasure than I care to admit. It starts this fever inside my body, charging me with an electrical current that makes me feel like a supervillain.

I need all the energy I can get right now. I try to contain it.

My body and brain switch back and forth between obsessing over the extreme thirst and dwelling on the gut-twisting hunger. Both ravage me down to the core of my soul. The faucet has gone dry. When it happened, I cried. Then I tried to dismantle it to use as a weapon, but without a screwdriver or some sort of tool, it proved impossible. Then I hated myself for wasting water on tears.

I wander across the room like a hollowed-out shotgun shell and sit in front of the collection of items lined up neatly on the floor. I start with the stack of drawings, counting them out. Then I move on to the notebooks, count them next. I continue down the line, counting everything I've taken from those cabinets. I've done it a hundred times to pass the time, and I'll probably do it one hundred more.

I stare at the contents of someone else's life, like the ghost of Clay is all around me.

I feel the whisper of his presence gliding across my skin, wondering if it's real or if I'm just going insane and my imagination is plunging over the edge.

"Help me." The words are nothing more than a flutter off my lips. I don't realize I'm crying silent tears until the dampness on my cheeks makes my face cold.

Sniffling, I press my forehead to my knees, my shoulders shuddering. "Please help me."

I don't even know who I'm talking to. If there is a sign, if there is some spirit of Clay left in this room and he can help me, I tap into it now, wanting to drink it in like a current of electricity going through a cord.

A heaving breath explodes from my chest, and my eyes burst open, my head tilted toward the ceiling.

"Help me!" I roar like a freight train, my voice bouncing off the walls, which are closing in on me.

The scream absorbs the rest of the energy that I have for right now. I crawl to the bed and get in, folding into the sheets like a turtle retreating into its protective shell. All that pacing I did, all those crunches and air punches—I would never have the energy to do all that now.

I have the boot with me, my arms curled around it, clinging to it like it's my lifeline. It's my weapon. I have nothing else aside from a few children's books. I think about Catherine's left knee. Clay wrote those words and hid them. Maybe even as a small child, he understood that someone may come after him. What a sweet, intelligent boy. What a waste to keep him from the world.

Mark told me Catherine had knee surgery six years ago. It was before we met. I never really processed the information. I've never noticed her limp, not once. But there's a chance that her left knee still troubles her, at least enough to drop her like a ton of bricks.

The thought helps me fall asleep in an optimistic frame of mind. Catherine is not going to leave me down here until I die. I know she won't. I just have to wait for her weaknesses to betray her.

Then I'll really hit her where it hurts.

CHAPTER THIRTY-TWO

Time is just fragments in my mind, chunks of space where I float between consciousness and unconsciousness. Every part of my body feels like it's been soaked in a vat of concrete. My eyelids are so heavy that I can barely keep them open anymore. My brain is functioning but not much else. It wills my arms to move. It urges my legs to push forward and get out of the bed. But the more and more time that passes, the harder and harder it gets for me to do these simple tasks.

I'm not even going to the bathroom anymore. There's nothing to flush out anymore. My body is empty. My brain is foggy. There's no light behind my eyes. My head throbs in a piercing migraine from starvation.

I'm too weak to even cry, but I feel the sobs, like a dormant volcano in my chest, ready for eruption, bubbling just under the surface.

I lift my head, but I'm too weak to do much else. When I stare at the ceiling, it looks like it's moving. I think I'm hallucinating. I see shadows in the corners of the room. Sometimes, I hear a muffled voice, but I know it's not there. It's just my mind descending into the madness created from solitude and starvation.

I lose track of just how long I've remained in this bed. I'm sewn to the mattress, my hair solidifying with the pillow. The shape of my body is indented forever into sheets. I forget how to move. I stop bothering to lift myself into a sitting position. There's no point. I have nowhere to go anyway, nothing to eat or drink.

I count my ragged breaths. It's the only way I can be certain I'm even still alive. My mind hangs on, but my heartbeat is low and quiet in my chest.

My body will give up soon. I'm hanging on for dear life, literally. A haze envelops me in mind, body, and spirit. I succumb to the fatigue.

I go through periods of dreamless sleeps in which I'm absorbed into a blank, black nothingness, like I've already died, like I'm lying still in my coffin, the small breaths I'm taking fading into nothing until there are none left at all.

But other times, I have periods of vivid dreams in which my brain refuses to give up and lets me know it's still fighting for its life, to keep me alive.

In these dreams, I see my parents. I wonder if it means I'm nearing the afterlife, if I'll soon be reunited with them. I feel my father's protective arms cloaked around me and the whisper of my mother's laughter tickling my cheek. These are wholesome dreams for me, like being wrapped in a warm hug or sinking into a warm bath.

I don't like it when I wake up and realize it's all been a dream. I want to go back to that amber light inside my head, where my mother's glinting eyes are smiling at me, welcoming me to a place where I'll no longer feel pain or hunger or sadness.

Then it happens. I start to lose hope. In fact, I welcome

death. Death is peace, and what I'm experiencing right now is the opposite. It's hell.

It's in the very moment I give up that I also hear a scratching noise. It's followed by a clicking sound. Both sounds are loud enough to capture my attention, and I turn my head in the direction they're coming from.

The door.

The sounds are coming from the *door*.

I find strength from deep within me.

I remove the sheets from my legs and reach out toward the floor. My palms hit the concrete, my fingers sprawled. One knee is on the floor now then the other. My eyes are fixated on the door, the sound of a lock grinding against a key.

The doorknob rattles then twists.

My pulse quickens for the first time in a long while, and heat washes through me. Blood rushes to my head.

I crawl, too weak to stand, the boot clutched in the crook of my elbow.

My breathing is hollow in my throat, a raspy sound that escapes my lips. I don't take my eyes off the door, but it's glitching in my vision, twitching, moving. My mind is boggy like the bottom of a swamp. Gravity pulls me down, making my body too heavy to move at more than a slug's pace across the room.

But I make it.

I'm at the door, on my knees, when it swings open.

I taste blood in the back of my throat. It's scratchy with thirst.

Catherine looms over me. I blink up at her. It takes my eyes a few moments to bring her whole body into focus. Her silver hair is pinned up into an impeccable bun. A string of pearls decorates her slender neck. Her manicured fingers are coiled around something shiny.

Squinting, I blink. She's carrying a box of more casserole dishes. Her eyes travel across me, and I watch the shock wander across her features, watch her eyes grow as wide as two newly hatched eggs as she takes in my form, inspecting me in my decrepit despair, my filth, my stench, my sunken cheeks and limp body.

I watch her shoulders lift and hear her sharp intake of breath. She slowly exhales, her throat bobbing. Her sleek fingers tighten around the box. Her brown eyes inspect me with horror for the state of my appearance. I barely have the energy for a smirk, but the edges of my lips tug upward anyway, unable to be contained.

Catherine's fingers slink across the top of the box and link around the handgun resting on top of it. It takes everything I have to raise myself into a standing position. I'm huffing as if I've just run a marathon. My cheeks burn as if my face is made of smoldering ash, ready to disintegrate.

I look at the gun then at Catherine.

She watches me watching her watching the gun. She clocks my every move, and I do the same to her. Neither of us says a single word.

I don't look like much of a threat to Catherine in my bent position, but she's looking at the boot with a perplexed wrinkle in the creases near her eyes.

Catherine begins to bend and puts the box down just inside the room, right by the door. I watch the indifference move over Catherine's face like blinds being shut, and I know this might be the only chance I get to freedom.

My legs barrel forward. I'm like a fawn first learning to walk, all limbs, wobbly on my feet. Catherine realizes what

I'm doing and draws the gun up toward my face, trying to take aim.

Gripping the boot, I pull it back over my shoulder, ready to bring it crashing down on her face. I take my swing, and the gun drops from Catherine's hand easier than I expected it to. She cries out in surprise, scrambling to retrieve it, but while her vulnerability is exposed, I make my next move.

Catherine is stumbling back on her heels, her arms extended and her body bending to pick up the gun, but I'm too fast for her. I swat the boot in her direction. She gives up on her mission to retrieve the gun and backs into the hallway. My heart slows, as does Catherine's motion as I realize she's going to lock me back in here, abandoning the gun. She has to make that choice, either to keep the door open or lose the gun. She can't have it both ways.

I can't let her lock me in here again. She might not come back a second time once this new food runs out.

She won't win. I won't let her.

Mind over matter, full-fledged survival instincts kick into gear, surging through me. I grit my teeth and scream. Catherine is sealing the door. The space is narrowing into just a slice between me and freedom, between me and that hallway behind her. I can't let it get away from me.

I shove the boot into the gap before she has a chance to slam the door shut.

CHAPTER THIRTY-THREE

Catherine's mouth collapses into an oval of shock. Her brown eyes stare at me, dazed and wide, the whites like snow against the darkness in the hallway. Her chest rises and falls in rapid succession as she draws in deep breaths, her bottom lip twitching, giving away just how much she underestimated me.

Catherine coils both hands around the doorknob. Her jaw clenches. The tendons in her neck bulge, and her eyes pinch into a grimace. She pulls, yanks, and grunts, trying as hard as she can to close the door in my face, but I've collected the shrapnel of strength deep within me, and now it's bashing down on her like a clap of thunder.

She groans again as she uses every ounce of strength in her body to pull on the door. Beads of sweat shimmer above her brow.

"Give up, old woman," I say. "Stop."

My voice has changed. It's lower and has a growl to it.

I yank and shove, gritting my teeth against the pain, against the energy it's taking to do this, and feel it zap from my bones as I cuff my fingers over the side of the door, willing it open, refusing to let her slam it on my knuckles.

Catherine gets a burst of energy herself, and the door pushes against the boot, nearly cracking it in half as she hucks her leg back and kicks the boot out from the wedge in the door.

"Give it up, Catherine," I pant. I'm not surrendering. I'm too close to that hallway, and I want to see what's on the other side. "I won't die in here like Clay."

Catherine doesn't respond, but I can hear her frantic swells of breathing. I belt out the deepest, most haunting, eardrum-shattering scream I can muster. It feels powerful, exploding from my chest like a bomb detonating. The release of it is ecstasy. I scream Clay's name right in her face.

It's enough to startle Catherine. She stares at me with terror in her eyes. I'm a feral monster, not the weak and timid daughter-in-law she expected.

Her grip on the doorknob slackens. Another guttural scream bursts from my throat again, and I yank as hard as I can. Catherine loses control of the door handle. She stumbles backward as the door flies open. I'm out in the hallway in a split second, before she can even blink.

In the dark hallway, we're a tangle of bodies, limbs, and flustered breathing.

Catherine shoves me. I claw at her face. She screams as my nails leave red track marks down the side of her cheek.

I grab her stupid fucking silver bun and yank her head back, pulling her to the floor. Then I'm off again, but Catherine takes a fistful of my hair and snatches it, sending me toppling into her heaving chest.

I spin around. Her jaw is flexed, eyes narrowed and burning. Her hair is askew, the pin loosened. Her neat bun is falling apart, just like her life.

She stands there with her mouth turned down with rage, her chin trembling and her hands quivering. Her eyes are murderously bloodshot and red rimmed. I raise my hand to punch her, but I waited a beat too long. Her fist reels back and barrels into the center of my face, knocking the breath from my lungs. A numb sensation travels through my nose before the pain cleaves my face. I gasp then belt out another roar. I taste blood and feel its wetness oozing down my nose, trickling across my lips, and sliding onto my tongue.

Instinctively, I bring my hand to my nose and cup my palm over it. When I draw it back, it's filled with a thick, syrupy crimson liquid.

Fury ignites inside me. I'm on my knees, my hands scrambling across the floor to fetch the boot. I manage to swipe it, and while I'm down, while Catherine is trying to shove me back into my eternal prison, my living hell, I crash the boot down on her bad left knee.

Catherine lets out a piercing scream of agony and collapses to the floor, her hands clutching her knee.

"You bitch!" she shouts, her angry voice filling the space between us, booming off the narrow hallway as spittle flies from her gnarled lips.

I don't even look back, just take off along the narrow corridor. *Where the hell am I?* This needs to lead to the basement, but I soon hit a dead end. My body smacks into the wall. I fan my fingers out like antennae, scrambling for a door, a latch, anything.

My hand hits something round, so I slip my fingers around it and look upward. *A ladder rung.* Smiling, I put one foot onto the ladder, testing the support, then raise one hand farther up, to the next rung. Halfway up, a wooden box, like a wine pallet, hits my back. I don't pay much attention but see that it's connected to a rope. That must be how she lowered me down as well as how she brought the food down.

A moment later, Catherine's huffing breaths and quickened steps come from behind me, so I pick up the pace, groaning against my ankle pain as I continue my ascent to what I hope and pray will be freedom.

When I've almost reached the top of the ladder, my injured foot slips, the cast slowing me down. My ankle throbs as it bangs into the rung that I just slipped from. I wince, biting my tongue and letting out a yelp of pain.

I take a shuddering breath and grip the ladder with my damp palms. I can't allow this to slow me down. Catherine is on my heels now, coming up the ladder. But she's slow too. I can hear her panting, and I see her struggling with her hurt knee.

Limping my way up, I try not to misstep again.

Anger is my fuel. Revenge is my strength. I'm doing this for Clay and for me.

Cold, bony fingertips snake around my good ankle, scratching at my heel. My heart is hammering in my chest. If she pulls me off the ladder, we'll both fall. *How far up am I now? Ten feet?* This has to be it, surely. There can't be much more to go.

I shake my leg, snatching myself out of her grip, and keep going.

Don't look down.

You're almost there, Jess.

Catherine swipes at my heels again.

She's closing in.

CHAPTER THIRTY-FOUR

My fingers fumble across the floor above me, and once I realize it's level footing, I start scrambling on my hands and knees until I can stir up enough energy to stand. I need to move, but I take several heaving breaths. My lungs are on fire, the air smoldering through my throat. I push my oily hair from my eyes and keep crawling, giving my throbbing ankle a break, but I don't know how much time I have before she catches up to me.

There's a scuffling sound. She's behind me, chasing me, but I don't know how close she is. I won't look back. I can't. This is it. Either I get out, or I'm dead. There's no going back in that hole now. She'll have to kill me to get rid of me.

I try to stand, and every part of my body is in agony. Hobbling, I put most of my weight on my good leg. I'm in the basement now, with the cluttered piles of junk all around me. But I know my way to the staircase, so I get on my hands and knees again, raising myself one step at a time, scrambling, frantic, my heart bashing against my ribcage.

I dare to steal a look behind me.

Catherine is a few feet away, her face contorted in rage.

Her teeth are bared, her fists balled and her knuckles white. My heart drops into my stomach when I see what's in her hands. She's got the gun. She must have grabbed it while I was on the ladder. And now she's trying to steady herself and her breathing enough to aim and shoot.

This time, I don't doubt she'll have the courage to pull the trigger to stop me.

I stand, wincing against the pain, and weave up the stairs, making myself a harder target to hit. But I'm not moving fast enough. With a guttural cry, I reach the top of the steps, urgency flooding my veins again. It's enough to keep me moving, but it's almost like being drunk. Wooziness makes me sluggish, making my head spin. I can't focus on anything. The door in front of me comes and in and out of my vision. But I somehow find the handle and push as the sound of a bullet ricochets around the basement below.

Fuck.

She actually pulled the trigger. Catherine is really trying to murder me now. But I slam the door shut behind me and turn the lock on the handle.

"Jessica!" she screams, banging her fists against the wood. The door shivers against her bucking and thrashing.

The knob jangles and jiggles as I back away.

"I'll shoot through the door," she warns me.

I take her word for it.

Wiping the sweat off my face and the back of my neck, I gasp, pausing a moment to catch my breath. Then I reach for the side table and drag it toward the door to block Catherine from opening it. It snags on the corner of a rug, and I curse before a bang and a splintering of wood sounds.

She meant it. She shot in the lock. But the table is in place, holding her back. The bullet whizzed through the air a few feet away from my hip.

I was lucky.

Get out, I think.

I turn around and tumble toward the kitchen door, groping the wall to keep my knees from buckling underneath my weight. Dark spots fill the edges of my eyeline, but I keep going, pushing through the dizziness and the pain throughout my body.

I can do this. Catherine isn't behind me. Another gunshot rings through the air, and now I know she's forcing her way through the door. I don't have long.

Half leaning against the wall, I make it out of the kitchen and down the hallway. In the struggle, I must have cut myself, because I'm leaving smudges of blood all over the walls. *Good.* If she kills me, at least I'll leave evidence here. *Try and wash this away, bitch,* I think.

Then I remember. There's a landline in the office. My pulse hammers against the base of my skull. This is it. My way to get help.

Unless... unless she moved it, hid it, or disconnected it.

But I have to check. It's worth the risk. I hurry into the room and close the door behind me. There's no point locking it because she'll just shoot the lock, but I manage to drag a cabinet across, limping on my cast. Just as the entryway is blocked, I hear her footsteps coming down the hall.

I back away and hurry over to the built-in bookcases. The phone is there on a lower shelf. I lift the receiver, noticing the wire is plugged into the wall, and call 911. Catherine is banging on the door. I try to block out the sounds of her fists pounding the wood.

The operator answers through a crackly receiver after three rings.

"Hello," I say in a breathless rasp. My throat is so dry I can barely speak. "I need help. My mother-in-law is trying to kill me."

The operator is female, and her voice is calm. She's trying to pry all this information out of me that I can't answer. I don't have time to elaborate on the details.

I recite a hasty address.

"Please. Please come quickly. She's going to kill me, and I'm already hurt. I don't know how much longer I can hold on. She has a gun. And she starved me. I keep almost passing out. This is... it's not good. I..."

The operator is asking me where I'm hurt, how I'm hurt, and where my mother-in-law is. Her voice is muffled. My brain is on the brink of giving up. I can't make sense of anything else. Words have no meaning. Her voice might as well be a million miles away and spoken in a language I can't understand.

The doorknob jiggles. I can hear her pressing her weight against the door, pushing the cabinet inch by inch. I didn't choose a heavy-enough object. She's going to get in. I have no time left. I have to get out of this house now.

I drop the phone while the dispatcher is calling out to me. Then I turn to the window at the back of the office. This one is not painted shut.

"Jessica," Catherine says, "let me in, and we can talk about this like civilized people. I'm not sure why you have this insane idea that I'm trying to hurt you. You're the one who refused to eat and shower. You're the one who made all this a complete and utter mess."

I shove the window open and pull over a chair to help me up. I don't know what Catherine is doing, but I assume it's some way to trick the 911 operator. She's trying to manipulate her way out of this yet again.

"Stop lying!" I grab the window, turn the handle, and

shove it as hard as I can, screaming to mask the sound of the hinges creaking.

"I'm not lying, sweetheart!" Catherine shouts through the door. "You're delusional. The sooner you accept that, the better."

Rain patters against the window, running in thin rivulets down the pane. It's stiff. The hinges are old, probably iron, and won't budge. I shoulder it, my eyes trained on the office door. Catherine is still pushing her weight against it. The cabinet is moving, snagging against the carpet.

She's weak, I realize. It would be open by now if she weren't. But I still don't have much time.

I step onto Nicholas's office chair, wincing from ankle pain. This is not going to be easy. But at least I'm going to land on a bed of soft flowers, nothing too thorny.

"Jessica, are you still there? Can you hear me?" the operator asks.

"I'm here!" Then I add loudly for the sake of the 911 call, "I'm hiding from my mother-in-law because she has a gun. You're unhinged, Catherine. You kept me locked in a hidden room for weeks. And you did the same thing to Clay, a seven-year-old child. You should be in jail, you monster!"

"Deluded!" Catherine yells.

Fuck her. I haven't hated anyone so much in my entire life. Even if the bones of Nicholas Hawley crawled their way out of his grave and strode into the office, I don't think I would hate anyone as much as I hate Catherine.

And with that, I throw my weight at moving the window up, the stiff hinges screaming in protest. Finally, I can fit my body through the gap. The cast thumps against the sill on my way down, then my shoulder slams into Catherine's plants, squashing them into the soft earth.

I ignore the pain throbbing from my ankle and crawl onto

the lawn in the backyard. Stumbling, I limp my way around the side of the house, my skin damp from the rain. Or maybe tears. I don't know. Both, probably.

The drive comes into view. I stumble across the gravel like a zombie, my balance top-heavy, a low growl of pain throttling from my throat. I almost fall. The road seems so far away. *Then what?* Catherine doesn't have a car, and Mark's is stuck in the garage. I force myself to move faster, but the cast trips me up as I transfer from the gravel drive to Catherine's front lawn. The grass is damp when I crumble like paper to my knees.

I force myself up onto my knees again, grunting against the pain. *Don't give up now, Jess.* My legs are leaden, barely keeping me upright. The world spins around me. I'm struggling to stumble back to the driveway, somehow getting off course. I need to get to the main access road. The police are on their way. I just need to wait for them.

A scream rips through the air, and my stomach sinks. I stagger back and flit my eyes toward the house to gauge how far away she is from me. Catherine's on the porch, jogging down the steps, her feet slapping against the wood planks. She scurries across the lawn and raises her pistol, the silver flashing against the gray sky.

I hold my breath and freeze, every muscle in my body tight. The moment stretches. It could be one second or even less before I move. I spin, forcing my body to work as I rush to the road, but then the gun fires, and a sharp pain erupts in my shoulder. I cry and lurch forward, landing on my knees. Pain burns my shoulder, spreading wildfire through the rest of my back.

I gasp for air, and I can't see straight. Scrambling across the grass, I leave a trail of blood behind me. I make it to a group of Catherine's tacky lawn ornaments near the edge of the lawn.

A teal glass orb is staked into the ground by a birdbath. I pluck it from the ground as Catherine's footsteps gain on me. She's aiming the gun at my heart. As soon as she's within reach, I stab the glass orb's spike into her bad knee.

Catherine wails in pain and stumbles back, rocking on her heels, her legs eventually giving out on her. She crashes to the ground on her ass, her legs sprawled out, a startled expression on her face.

The gun goes off again when she hits the ground, the bullet firing into the sky. I scream. She cries out. I have no idea where the bullet goes and brace for impact, but it never happens. My shoulder throbs. My left arm is numb.

Before Catherine can get up again, I push her chest with my good palm. She shouts, startled. I'm on top of her, straddling her as she's lying like a starfish on the grass. We're both panting hard. Sweat is in my eyes, salty and burning. My hair is a matted mess in front of my face.

I swipe the strands away and raise the spiky stake of the lawn ornament over my head. Catherine's eyes grow wide with horror as she realizes what I'm getting ready to do. She tries to scramble away from me, wiggling and thrashing, but I squeeze my thighs against the sides of her torso to prevent her from going anywhere.

I bring the stake end down onto her chest, plunging the sharp end deep into her breastplate, and I wince as I hear her bones cracking. I twist the spike, but I get resistance from more bone, probably her ribs.

I pull the spike out and slam it down again in the same place. Blood spurts out like a fountain, spraying across my face and hers. Catherine is trying to scream, but it comes out as a gurgle. Blood bubbles pop in her mouth as she parts her lips in a strangled scream.

Her eyes lose their glossy sheen. Next, her skin pales, turning as white as linen, before it settles on an ashen gray like the sky. She tries to speak but instead chokes.

Heaving, I yank the spike from her chest. I can't feel the side of my body where the bullet hit my shoulder. My blood drips down my arm and my back like water dribbling down a rocky brook.

Tires crunch on gravel. I'm still on top of Catherine. I turn my head ever so slightly. Then my heart sinks when I realize it's not a patrol officer or an ambulance. It's a rental car, and Mark is in the driver's seat, his mouth hanging open, horror etched onto his face. Eyes of shock and anger burn straight into me.

I drop the lawn spike and peel myself off Catherine, collapsing to the grass beside her in a bloody, messy heap.

CHAPTER THIRTY-FIVE

Muffled footsteps scurry over the grass to where I'm lying with Catherine.

She isn't moving. I think she's dead, but I can't tell. Though I saw the life leaving her eyes, I didn't witness her taking her last breath.

Mark speaks, but his voice is so muted I can barely make out the words. He falls to the ground beside Catherine and wails with grief. I'm too exhausted to react.

I tilt my head to see my husband and witness his expression twisted in agony, fat tears streaming down his face. His hands are covered in Catherine's blood. He raises them, shaking.

When his tortured eyes meet mine, I'm not prepared for it. The scathing hatred and wrath that smolders there takes my breath away. I question every decision I've made leading up to this awful moment. But I can't take it back now. His nostrils flare, his teeth bared, his jaw clenched tight, and his shoulders rising quickly.

"*What did you do?*" His voice thunders through the space

between us. The veins in his neck are like bulging rivers, the tendons like cords ready to snap.

His face is red. "*What did you do?*" he roars.

I'm drifting in and out of consciousness. At this point, I can't even lift my head anymore. I'm exhausted. I did what I had to do. It was either me or her. Self-defense. I had no other choice. She shot me, and I'm bleeding out. I might not survive after all this.

My senses are dull, but I'm able to hear Mark's wails of despair and sorrow. They penetrate through me. He picks up his mother's torso and cradles her limp body in his arms. Mark presses her head to his chest and cries, his entire body shaking. He rocks her. She looks so frail and innocent, a far reach from the monster she was in life.

I stretch my fingers across the grass. It's the most I can do. I'm able to touch the tips of them to the fabric of his jeans. But he doesn't notice. He doesn't even look at me, just cradles and rocks his dead mother.

With the way he has her head tilted, I can see the part of her face that's not mushed into his chest. Her eyes are still open, staring at me, vacant.

I look away, bile rising in my throat. I don't even have the energy to cry. Mark hasn't noticed the gun or the bullet hole in my shoulder.

I gaze up at the canopy of trees. The limbs and leaves droop toward me. The sky feels like it's caving in on me. Soon, the trees will crush me with their weight, covering me with their branches until I am nothing, until I am forgotten.

At least I eliminated the threat. At least Catherine is gone. The effects of her torture still ripple like a splash in a lake, but at least she can't hurt anyone else ever again.

I did it for me, but I also did it for Clay.

* * *

Shrill sirens pierce my eardrums. Red and blue lights flash against tree trunks, shimmering against the damp grass.

A low moan escapes my throat. Movement rushes across the grass. Mark shouts that his wife killed his mother.

A man exclaims that they found a gun in the grass. Someone is kneeling over me. It's not Mark. It's a police officer. His bulletproof vest is bulky and boxy across his torso, and it has a million gadgets strapped to it. He says something into the radio attached to a loop on the vest. I can't make it out. I can only hear the static crackles.

He kneels in front of me, lifts my limp arm, and pushes two fingers into the sensitive flesh in the back of my neck.

When he scans me, his eyes widen at seeing the bullet hole oozing blood from my shoulder.

"Younger female has a pulse!" he shouts behind him.

People in white shirts and blue gloves roll a stretcher across the grass. They amble to my side.

"This one's deceased," a man declares grimly.

Mark lets out a low moan.

"Is this the murder weapon?" a woman asks.

I whimper again. I'm too weak to speak or move.

"Stabilize her neck before we move her," one of the male paramedics says.

"We're going to have to read her her rights first," the male officer who had crouched to take my pulse says, raising his chin toward his fellow first responders.

"You can do so and follow us to the hospital to obtain custody," the paramedic says in a flat voice. He has one of those oxygen things in his hand, pumping it with his fingers. He puts it over my face, and a rush of cold air sweeps into my nostrils and my mouth.

I inhale a sharp breath. Then I feel a prickle against the vein in my elbow and flinch. I'm lifted onto the stretcher on the count of three. A woman holds an IV bag over her head, running back to the ambulance with me on the stretcher, the wires and tubes connected to the IV port they just sank into my arm.

I moan in pain. Every muscle and bone aches, like they're broken, ripped apart. Every movement, bump, and jolt in the stretcher is agony. I'm stabilized in a neck brace. Someone is tending to my bullet wound. I scream in pain. My stomach churns, and my vision blurs. I black out, a welcome relief from this nightmare.

* * *

I wake up to a piercing fluorescent light beating down on me from the ceiling, and I blink, trying to clear the haze in my eyes.

My throat is still dry and gritty, but I feel more clear-headed. I try to raise my arm to scrub it over my face, but it doesn't move. When I glance down, I realize with horror that my wrist is handcuffed to the side of the hospital bed.

Terror squeezes my throat, and I start to hyperventilate, trying to sit up straight. I'm wearing a hospital gown and nothing else. An IV is still attached to my arm, the tubes winding up to a bag on a stand beside the bed.

I start breathing hard and fast, yanking on the handcuff.

No. Not again. This can't be happening. Catherine is dead. She can't be doing this to me.

"No... No... Catherine can't... she can't hurt me... no handcuffs... not a prisoner..." I speak in frantic whispers, yanking and pulling, but I'm not able to formulate a sentence that makes sense.

Someone jumps up from a chair in the corner of the room and bolts to the door. My heart collapses and explodes. It's Mark. He's wearing gray sweatpants and a white T-shirt that's one size too small and accentuates his slim frame and the cords of his muscles as he moves.

"She's awake, Officer!" he exclaims, poking his head into the hallway.

I swallow hard, blinking my husband into focus. He looks taller and leaner. His hair seems darker. His eyes are red rimmed and bloodshot. His mannerisms are panicked as he cuts a nervous glance at me over his shoulder.

A police officer with a potbelly steps into the room. He brings a fist to his mouth and coughs into it then hikes up his pants. The radio on his vest crackles, and he twists a knob to shut it off.

My spine straightens like an arrow, and all my sore muscles freeze, aching in protest. The officer's badge plate reads Harper. He's clean-shaven and has a baby face with rosy cheeks. He barely looks twenty-five years old.

"Mrs. Hawley?"

I swallow. "Am I under arrest?"

The officer keeps his attention on me even though Mark steps up beside him.

"You're in custody for now, yes. My body camera will be recording our conversation."

Tears pool in my eyes for the first time since everything happened. I bite my bottom lip to keep it from quivering too much. "I had to do it."

Officer Harper tilts his head. "What do you mean?"

Mark sucks in a sharp, deep breath.

Officer Harper finally looks at him. "Mr. Hawley, would you mind stepping outside for a minute so we can talk?"

Mark's eyes widen. "You're kidding me, right? My wife just killed my mother. I need to know why."

Harper rubs his jaw and parts his legs, clearly leveling his patience. Then he swivels back to me. His eyes are blue and creased with kindness.

"Detective Smithfield is on his way. We're going to ask you a few questions about what happened. Anything you can remember. We'll do it right here while you rest and recover."

He sounds too nice for the situation. Mark picks up on it too.

"Are you kidding me? She just killed someone," he snaps.

"You don't know what it was like!" I cry out, startling myself and the two of them. Tears leak down my face then start streaming as if someone turned on a faucet behind my eyes. "She locked me in the basement."

Mark's mouth drops open.

Harper nods, gives me a sympathetic look, and says, "Okay, we'll talk about it. We'll figure it all out."

Just as he says it, a tall man walks through the door. He has red hair and a red mustache to match. He's wearing a tan suit that is a little too long at the wrists and ankles. His detective badge flashes against his breast pocket under the too-bright lights.

He approaches the bed, reaches out to shake hands with me, and introduces himself as Detective Smithfield. I reluctantly take his hand, which is a little clammy and warm.

Harper informs him, "She's saying the victim locked her in a basement."

Smithfield turns his attention to me. "How did you get out?"

I take a giant, heaving breath, and through my tears and sniffles, I explain everything that happened. I start from the beginning and leave nothing out, trying to remember as much as I can in as much detail as I am able to relay.

When I'm finished, I look at all three of them. Mark is staring at me in disbelief. The officers look calm. They probably hear horror stories like this all the time and have to act neutral until they have all the facts, until they have the proof either way.

The detective says he's going to step outside for a few minutes. The officer tells Mark and me that he'll be outside until he gets word from the forensics team and his boss on whether they will choose to take me to the station once I get clearance from my doctor. I secretly pray they'll find the basement and the fingerprints on her gun and they'll let me go.

"Will you please take the handcuff off?" I ask.

Harper doesn't hesitate. He reaches over the side of the bed and unlocks it. "We had to do that as a precaution to make sure you wouldn't be a danger to yourself or the hospital staff once you woke up."

I rub the soreness out of my wrist and look down. "Thank you."

"You're not being discharged yet. They're monitoring you. We'll let you know once we get word later from the forensics team and the officers and your admitting doctor."

"Okay," I whisper, hating how meek I sound and how undecided my fate still is.

Harper exits the room. The only sounds are his footsteps on the linoleum floor padding away. He quietly shuts the door behind him, leaving me alone with a husband who hates me.

When it's only Mark and me left in the room, he exhales slowly just as I'm breathing in a breath of dread. It's too quiet. Mark is staring at the floor.

"Mark... it was self-defense."

He raises his head, and it breaks my heart to see the pain on his face, the agony in his eyes, and his watery lashes.

"I'm so sorry," I whisper. "I know you loved her."

His throat bobs. He presses his lips together then opens them. "You... she really... she locked you in the basement? That there's a tunnel..."

I nod.

Mark shakes his head as if to clear it, but his expression remains dumbfounded. He kneads the back of his neck. "It sounds ridiculous. Made-up."

"Well, it's not," I snap. "And when the police find it all, you'll change your tune." I shake my head. "Look at me, Mark. Look at me. She tried to starve me. I haven't had a shower in weeks. *Look at me!*"

He winces. Silence stretches between us.

I sniffle quietly, fuming but also saddened to a depth I didn't think I could reach.

Eventually, curiosity gets the better of me, and I ask, "Why are you here? Why did you come back from Japan?"

He finally regards me as if he's just seeing me for the first time. "How long were you down there?"

"I don't know. I lost track of the days. At first, I wrote them on the wall. Like a tally. But it didn't last long. I was out of my mind. I just slept and ate and did some exercise. Looked through Clay's journals. Eventually, the food ran out. I got so weak I couldn't leave the bed anymore." I pause as another swell of emotion claims me, and the tears spring back to my eyes.

"And Clay is a boy that used to be locked down there. You said he was my brother when you were talking to the police."

I turn and stare at him, knowing my eyes are hard. "Yes. Clay is the little boy your parents kept locked there when you were a child. I think he was your parents' biological child."

He takes a step back. "It's crazy."

"Your mother was a monster." I bite my lip. I can't tell Mark about the hospital swap, not here, not like this.

He rakes his fingers through his hair. Then he shakes his head, and I feel like he's dismissing me, that he thinks I'm a crazy woman making it all up.

Mark reaches for a tissue and hands it to me. Then he says, "I came home early. I started to catch on that something wasn't right."

My eyebrows rise. "You did? I... I mean... I thought you might. Eventually. I had no idea what kind of lies she might have been feeding you."

"Quite a few big ones, it turns out." Mark rocks back on his heels, a muscle feathering in his jaw.

He shoves his hands into his sweatpants pockets. Then he pulls one out and scratches the top of his head, blowing out a puff of air as if he needs a moment to figure out how to say what he's going to admit next.

"Everything is just so messed up." His chin quivers. Despite his lack of support, I want to hug him close and feel the rhythm of his heart beating against my ear, pulsing against my cheek. "Are you... are you sure about everything?"

"Do you want to see the bullet hole?" I ask.

He shakes his head. "She lied to me." His jaw clenches. "My whole life." His nostrils flare. "I had a brother, and I didn't even know it. She locked my wife in a basement and shot her. She was willing to let you die, starve to death in there. If she didn't end up dead, too, I hope she would rot for what she did."

"Mark..."

"No, it's true." His eyes are glazed with ice, but this time, it's not meant for me. "She deserves what she got." Then his eyes soften, and he finally takes my hand. "I should have seen the warning signs. I should have known. I should have protected you and been more available. I should never have left you with her."

"Don't talk about all the should-haves. It's not worth it." I can't deny that his initial suspicions hurt my already wounded heart, but I can see him finally beginning to accept the truth. I squeeze his hand.

Mark sniffles and looks at the ceiling to keep his tears from spilling over. "She made me believe you were leaving me, feeding me all these lies about how unhappy you were, about how she would take care of me and I could rely on her. She manipulated me into thinking my own wife hated me. Your absence left a huge hole in my heart that I knew nothing would be able to fill. I had to find out for myself. I was desperate to see you and talk to you and find out why and what went wrong."

He sucks in a deep, ragged breath.

"I figured she would do something like that," I whisper. "To be honest, I never thought I'd see you again. I got to a point that I was so hungry and cold, so lost and alone, I started to give up on ever getting out of that room. I started to think about death a lot. I had dreams about my parents. They were so real. It was like I could actually reach out and touch them, talk to them, hold them."

Tears roll down Mark's face. He sits down on the edge of the bed and rubs his hand up and down my arm. The motion of his fingertips brushing my skin is soothing, healing.

"I came home early because I wanted to find you to try to convince you to stay with me and that we could get through this rough patch. That's when I pulled up to the house and saw you stabbing her with the lawn ornament."

It hits me then how jarring that moment must have been, to believe your wife is leaving you and won't speak to you, only to see her murdering your mother as you pull up to your house. "Fuck. I can't even imagine what that was like."

"The worst moment of my life," he says. "By far."

His eyes are far away. I wonder if we can get over this, together, as husband and wife. He saw me stabbing his mother. I learned the deepest, darkest, and vilest secrets about his family. *Is our love strong enough to survive this?*

Suddenly, Mark sits up straighter. "The figure in the room, the one my mother convinced me was just a bad dream—it was Clay. It had to be Clay."

I nod. "I read his journals. He tried to escape, and he ran up to find you. Oh, Mark, he was such a sweet child. Your mother would tell him all about you. I think he wanted to play with you. Or maybe save you from your parents."

Mark wipes the tears off his damp cheeks. "I'm glad I have the truth now. I love you so much, Jess."

He squeezes my hand. Then one finger gently pushes back my damp, dirty hair.

"I love you too." Then I add because I want it to be true, "We're going to get through this. I promise."

CHAPTER THIRTY-SIX

It's been two weeks since Catherine's death. I'm trying not to allow my brain to revisit all the brutal details of everything that happened, but it's difficult, especially since we're standing in the cemetery, next to her casket, before it gets lowered into the ground.

The funeral was small and low-key. Only a handful of her friends attended, and they've all gone home now. Mark didn't want to have a reception afterward. He just wanted to get it over with and not have to answer a lot of questions.

A few kind words were said on her behalf, but that was it. Not even Mark wanted to stand at the lectern next to her coffin and say anything. He just stares into the hole with a blank expression on his face. I'm worried about him and the way he's processing all this. No one seems to question his behavior, which is a relief. Everyone grieves in their own way, and they're probably assuming that's the way Mark is handling it internally.

We've talked about what happened in short bursts of conversation. It's as though any more would be too much for us to both take. But we did agree to keep everything that happened under wraps, at least as much as we can. Obviously, there's a police investigation into what happened. Some of it will come out. But it's not like there is anyone left to prosecute. Catherine is dead, and her husband has been gone a long time. It just leaves the mystery of Clay and what happened to him still up in the air.

The police chose not to charge me after they discovered the basement and found the proof that I'd been locked in that awful dungeon-like place.

Mark is a statue beside me. His posture is rigid, the muscles in his jaw flexed. He's glaring down at the hole in the ground, at the mahogany box containing the body of his mother—or the woman who claimed to be his mother, but as it turns out, she wasn't even related to him. I can't imagine the range of emotions he's going through right now. She might not have been his mother by blood, but she was the only mother he ever knew.

I put a hand on his back and rub the heel of my hand up and down his spine to calm him down. Mark doesn't look at me, but he licks his lips and nods, a slight acknowledgment that he knows I'm just trying to do anything I can that will comfort him.

I know he's still in pain, tortured by the revelations that have come to light, the terrible things Catherine did to him and his brother—to Lily and Steven. I told him everything once I was discharged from the hospital. When I recovered my phone from Catherine's room, I charged it and showed him Steven's emails and the photos he allowed me to see. Mark sat and cried for hours afterward, letting it all out—the pain of the betrayal and the grief of losing someone close, even if they were a shitty person.

I keep coming back to Catherine. Her brand of evil was inconsistent with the villains we see on television. She was an attentive mother to Mark. The journals showed her love for Clay and her affection for him. I get the sense that Catherine was not the ringleader in the Hawleys' circus of cruelty. But even if it wasn't her idea, even if her husband forced her to switch Mark at birth with her own baby, to lock Clay in a basement, she could have found a way to stop it all if she'd really wanted to.

Catherine could have found a way to confess, to go against him. She kept Clay locked in there because she didn't want him to get out either. She had taken it too far and probably knew he'd tell on her, and she couldn't risk it.

The evil was just brewing underneath the surface all those years, until her angst faded away into something that resembled confidence. By the time she met me, that confidence, that conniving mentality that she could get away with anything, sprouted high enough for her to be able to drug me, shove me into a dark room, and leave me there to wither away, pointing a gun at me to keep me in line.

So for Mark's benefit, we kept the details of her death vague. He told everyone it was an accident that happened in her front garden, which was technically a partial truth.

On the ride back to the house, it started to rain, just a light drizzle, but it was enough to sprinkle wetness across the windshield. Mark switched on the wipers. I watched the blades sweep across the glass back and forth, the rhythm of it hypnotizing and slightly lulling.

The police have finally gone. Cadaver dogs roamed the grounds, searching for Clay's body. They found nothing. The room below the basement has been turned over by a forensics team. Almost all of it has been dismantled and taken away.

Mark stares up at the red house. "My entire life was a lie."

"Mark, honey." I reach over the center console and knead the dip of his shoulder.

"No, it's true." He flicks his gaze to me then back to the road. His fingers squeeze tighter around the steering wheel. "My childhood was a lie, at least."

"You can't get it back, but you can move forward," I remind him. "We have our whole lives to be together to make new, happier memories that will last a lifetime."

Mark swallows and continues to stare at the house.

"I know you're upset about everything that's happened," I say. "We've both been through a lot. We need to stick together."

He turns to me again, his eyes roaming over my arm sling. I'll have to wear it for the next month. But at least the cast on my leg is finally off.

"You're right," he says, his tone softening. "Here I am, sitting in my own woes, when I should be caring for you after what she did to you."

"I'm just glad it's over. I want to try to move on now. And I want you to join me on that path."

He nods, scrubs a hand over his face, and takes a deep breath. "It will take some time, but I know what you mean."

I glance at my sling just as he looks at it again. "Sorry for the constant reminder that I have to wear for the next month."

"Right when you get your boot off, you get a new injury to replace it." Mark laughs, but the sound is wrapped in barbed wire, as if he doesn't find it funny at all.

"I'll be all right," I assure him. "It's only temporary. Like all of this." I gesture around, although I'm not sure he's getting my point. I'm not sure I even understand what I'm trying to say. All my thoughts and feelings feel blotched together, both dulled and fraying at the corners.

Mark barks a laugh, but his face is twisted into a grimace. He's still staring out the windshield. "My own mother wasn't even my mother. I'll never get to meet my real mother. All of that was robbed from me before I even had a chance."

The anger melds with the hurt in his voice.

"Maybe we can go meet your dad," I suggest, even though it feels weird saying it. "Your real dad."

Mark glances at me. "Steven?"

"Yeah."

He contemplates quietly for a few moments and shrugs. A sliver of a smile cracks at the corner of his mouth. "Sure. Yeah. Maybe."

The glimmer of hope in his eyes starts to grow. The rain falls harder now, and the wiper blades squeak against the windshield. The sound of the raindrops plunk on the top of the car and roll over the passenger window.

I watch it, thinking of new beginnings and the second chance at life I've been given. I know how lucky I am. Most stories like mine don't have good endings. I'll never take it for granted, or the fact that I escaped that prison, cheating death as it stared me in the face, chasing me down and trying to break me.

CHAPTER THIRTY-SEVEN

We're sitting in Steven's living room. It's quiet here, and the only sound is the clock ticking on the wall. I'm holding a mug of warm peppermint tea. But the air around us is cool. Mark is sitting on the couch beside me, his knee touching mine. It keeps bouncing up and down with nerves. And Steven is sitting in a chair across from us, a coffee table separating us from him. He's eyes flit from us to the ground and back again.

The silence stretches. Finally, Steven licks his lips, adjusts himself in the seat, opens his mouth, sighs, and scratches the back of his head. Then he leans forward and props his elbows on his knees, clamping his hands together.

"So, I'm glad to finally be meeting you," Steven says, his eyes on Mark.

Mark nods. "Yeah." His voice is too quiet. "Better late than never, right?"

This brings a small smile to Steve's mouth, but it's enough to reach his eyes. "Yeah. Better late than never."

Mark straightens his shoulders and clears his throat. "Jess showed me some baby pictures of you. We look a lot alike. Well, I think so. I mean, I saw resemblances."

"You still look a lot alike," I chime in. "There are more than just resemblances."

"If you want, I can show you more pictures." Steven flits his gaze between us, expectantly.

Mark and I exchange glances, and I wait for him to answer.

"Sure," Mark says, polite yet reserved. "Sure. Yeah. That sounds good."

Steven stands up. "I'll be right back." He looks between us. "Can I get you anything else? I can make sandwiches or something if you guys are hungry."

"I think we're okay for now." Mark looks at me. "Unless you want—"

"No, I'm fine. Thank you." I offer Steven a polite smile.

He looks relieved to see us on his couch, in his home. It's still hard to digest that this is Mark's real father standing beside us, but one step at a time is all we can handle for now.

"Just try to relax," I whisper once Steven is gone. "You're doing great."

Mark wipes the sweat off his temple and rubs his forehead. "I know. This is just... a lot."

"But at least you've met him now," I whisper. "That's the hardest part. Now you don't have to wonder anymore."

Mark nods, takes a deep breath, and blows it out. He looks like a deer in headlights, overwhelmed and not knowing what to do next.

"Why don't you drink some of your water?" I suggest. "You look a little pale."

Mark unscrews the lid, brings the bottle to his lips, and glugs down a few sips, swallowing noisily.

"There. That's better." I smooth out the creases in the back of his shirt with my palm, scratching my nails down his back the way he likes for comfort and support. "I'm right here. It will take a while for you guys to get to know each other, but I'm sure in time, you'll find things you have in common."

Mark smiles. "Thank you. You're seriously the best. I don't know what I'd do without you."

I cup his cheek. I can feel the love connection still between us. Mark might have been confused and upset when he saw what I did to Catherine, but he came home early from Japan. He knew in his gut that something wasn't right. And even now, he still wants me. Seeing him by my side, feeling his hand in mine, it all feels right. It feels good.

Steven returns, carrying the photo albums.

"Here are some good ones," he says, sitting them on the coffee table in front of us.

"Fantastic," I say, pick one up, and open it.

As we begin to thumb through the album, Steven talks about things he's done in his life, places he's been, foods he likes to eat, and what he did for a living before he retired. Mark starts to open up, too, telling more about himself. He asks questions about Lily, his real mother.

"She was a warm person," Steven says. "I think if she had a fault, it was that she loved too hard." His voice cracks, and he clears his throat. "She wanted you home, Mark. Don't get me wrong. She loved Freddy so much. We both did. Hell, I believed he was my son until the day he died. Lily loved you both like you were both hers." He wipes tears from his eyes. "I don't know what we would have done if we'd proved you were our child. I don't know if we could have just swapped you like that. Freddy made our lives... wonderful. He was special."

Mark nods. "I understand."

"Sorry," Steven says. "I'm not saying you weren't special too." He points at a picture of a smiling boy. "But there he is. Our Freddy."

I lean down to get a closer view. There she is—Catherine's features, her dark-amber eyes, her sharp nose. Freddy's face is Catherine's face. It almost alarms me. But he seems like a sweet child, smiling broadly next to a blue toy truck.

"I wonder what kind of life I would have had if the swap hadn't happened," Mark says.

"Well, I don't know for sure, but I do think my Lily would still be here. And she would have been just as good a mother to you as she was to Freddy." Steven smiles.

I brush tears from my cheeks. So many lives were destroyed because of the Hawleys and their terrible games.

"I still don't know why my mother... I mean Catherine... did these things," Mark says. "My father was a strict man. He barely spoke to me before he died. We ate every meal with him, and he would ask me about school then immediately get his newspaper to read. He wasn't... he wasn't like you, Steven." Mark pulls in a deep breath. "When he died, it was like the clouds parted to bring out the sun. I know I can't forgive my mother for what she did. But once he was gone, things were good."

I squeeze Mark's knee. "None of it is your fault."

"No," Steven says. "Your parents made terrible choices. But it doesn't erase your mother's kindness to you." He sighs. "For what it's worth, I don't hate her. I can't. She gave us Freddy, and I loved him. And now I get to know you too. The way it all happened was terrible, but I want to make it into something positive now."

Mark nods. "So do I."

I'm happy for them. I love that Mark has a second chance

with his real father. He never really had a dad growing up, just a distant, cruel man. And now he has Steven.

But I don't know if I can get on board with Steven's inability to hate Catherine. I still hate her for what she did to me, and I'm not sure that will ever change.

EPILOGUE

My heart drums hard as Mark pulls the car into the driveway. He doesn't shut off the engine. Instead, he keeps his hands clamped on the steering wheel, his face pale, a sheen of sweat glossing his forehead.

I give his shoulder a tender squeeze. "Mark, honey? Are you okay?"

He blinks and moves his head toward me as if snapping himself from a daze. Then he nods. "I think so."

"You can do this. I'm right here beside you."

He rubs his forehead, and I see him finally make the decision. He shuts off the engine and flits his gaze back to the house in front of us, sighing long and deep, like he's releasing all the air inside his body in one swoop.

My heart pounds. I don't tell Mark how nervous I am, but I'm sweating. For six months, we've searched for Clay. We read every diary in the house. Catherine never kept one, but we went through her notes. We ransacked Nicholas's office. We searched missing person reports. Then we went to the library and looked through archived police reports.

Finally, we found an address belonging to a man who

was once taken in by a driver a few miles from the Hawleys' house. The boy had Treacher Collins syndrome, which results in facial disfigurement. He was then adopted and moved around twenty miles outside of Mark's hometown. We finally tracked down Paul, who might just be Clay Hawley.

Clay means so much to me. His journals saved my life. As I read them, I wanted to hold this child who was treated so poorly by his parents. I still do, but now he's a fully grown man.

I look at the house in front of us. It's a French Tudor style, with green ivy crawling up the whitewashed brick on the side. A large oak tree hangs over the impeccably manicured lawn, the grass green and lush.

Mark licks his lips, declaring the same incantation I've been saying in my head the entire drive over here. "I can do this." He shakes his head and corrects himself. "*We* can do this. Together. Forever and always."

"Yes, we can. One step at a time."

Mark set up the meeting about a week ago. He said Paul sounded surprised and emotional on the phone. Now here we are, and there's no turning back. I have no idea whether Paul will be happy to see us or this will open old wounds that he'd prefer to keep closed.

Mark opens his car door, and I do the same. We walk together, fingers threaded, up the front-porch steps. He rings the doorbell, and we hear it chiming on the other side.

He tenses beside me as we hear footsteps approaching. We each suck in a breath simultaneously when the door swings open.

The man on the other side has eyes the color of a golden sunset. His dark hair is swept to one side, a little unruly but in waves like wheat in a field. My eyes tear up when I see him for the first time in the flesh, when my brain registers that he's real, that he's alive, that he made it out just like I did.

He's Clay, and he's here, standing before us, with a smile as wide as the ocean, as welcoming as a hug.

"Mark!" he says, opening his arms to pull his little brother to him.

Tears immediately well in my eyes when I see Mark fold into Clay's—no, Paul's—arms.

"Oh my goodness," Paul says. "I heard so much about you when I was little. I even saw you once. Come on. Come inside."

We follow him.

He's still talking, his voice full of excitement. "I can't believe you're finally here, Mark."

"In the flesh," Mark declares with a nervous chuckle.

"Come in. Come in. Make yourselves at home."

We choose spots on a comfy cream sofa, and I finally take Paul in. He's tall and broad shouldered and has dark hair and Catherine's eyes. But they're too far apart, drooping downward. His face is puffy, a little scarred, his mouth wide above a narrow chin. This is the face that Nicholas could not stand to look at. But all I see is Paul's warmth.

I swallow, trying to contain all the emotions bubbling to the surface. "Clay—sorry, Paul. I... I know you as Clay. It's so good to finally meet you."

Paul's eyes skim to me, and his smile grows impossibly bigger. "So *you're* the one who read through all my journals?" He laughs. "What do you think? Should I make them into a book?"

We all laugh, and it's like a rubber band popping inside me, stretched to its limit, finally snapping from the pressure.

"I'm sure it would captivate the masses," I say. "It's quite a tale."

THE MOTHER-IN-LAW

"One you endured yourself." Paul, sitting in the chair opposite, leans toward me and takes my hand. "It's so good to meet you, too, Jess."

"You saved my life, you know. That trick about hitting her in the knee. That's what got me out of that place."

Paul's expression morphs from happy to sad. He turns his head slightly, and I see the outline of a hearing aid behind his ear. He sniffs deeply and shifts his gaze back to mine. "So it's true. She's really gone?"

"She's gone," Mark says somberly.

Paul gives my hand one last squeeze then drops it. "It's so strange. Even after all these years and everything she did to me, I still miss her."

"That's understandable," I say, remembering those journals. Catherine took him treats, watched movies with him, and even stayed with him as he slept. That must have been like sunlight on a cold day to Paul.

He nods. "There were times I thought she genuinely loved me."

"I think she did," I say. "As fucked-up as that sounds."

He laughs.

I glance around the room, taking in a life lived. There's a wedding picture on top of the windowsill. His wife is pretty and petite with blond hair.

"That's Taylor," he says, smiling. "We went to school together." He walks over to the window and picks up the photo. "We were childhood sweethearts."

"I can't believe I missed your wedding," Mark says then laughs. "Of all the things to say."

"No, I get it," Paul says. "I missed yours too." He places the photo back in its spot. "I wanted to come back for you, you know. I hated leaving you there in that house. With Father especially."

"He died," Mark says. "Years ago now, when I was just a kid. Pancreatic cancer."

Paul raises his chin. "I wish I could say I'm sorry, but I'm not. I'm glad you weren't brought up by him."

"Can you tell us a little about how you escaped?" I ask.

Paul shivers. I see the trauma rising, but he pushes it down. I make a mental note to ask him how he did that.

"Well, I was about ten, I think. Mom used to tell me how old I was, but I never knew whether to believe her." He sighs. "It happened when you were at soccer camp, Mark. Father drove you there. Mom told me when it was going to be in advance because I think she wanted me to escape. She came down with pizza and a movie, and she stood there in the doorway, waiting. I kicked her hard in the knee and watched her fall. Then I grabbed the door and ran."

"I remember Mom seeming different when I came home from camp," he says. "She seemed... sad."

Paul brushes away a tear. "Maybe she was. I don't know. All I know is I ran to the road and kept running until I saw a car." He brushes away another tear. "The thing is I didn't actually run away. That wasn't what I wanted. I wanted to get... fixed. So I asked the man driving the car if he would take me to a hospital so they could fix my face. I thought if I did, Father might love me."

A gasp of sorrow escapes my lips. Without thinking, I reach forward and grasp Paul's hand. No child should want to fix their appearance in the hope that their parents might love them.

Paul smiles slightly, but it's filled with sadness.

Mark stands suddenly and paces the room. "I don't understand Father. Why did he care so much about... about having a perfect child?"

"We were possessions to him. Objects," Paul says. "Mom

told me everything when we were down in the basement room. *My* room, as I think of it. There is a Hawley tradition of babies being born at home. Father was born in the house his father built. His father was built in some other house, wherever they lived before. It was probably some outdated way of keeping their pregnant women bedbound." He lets out a derisive snort. "Anyway, when I was born, I was defective. At least, that's how Father saw it. I messed up the image he wanted for his family. Since he was a judge and a prominent man in the town, having a child who looked like me was... unthinkable to him. Mom caught him trying to smother me. That was when they decided to... well, you know the rest."

I close my eyes for a moment, trying to contain all the rage inside my body. Then I ask, "Was the room already there?"

He nods. "It was built as an underground bunker. They converted it into a room for a child."

I run my fingers through my hair, hardly able to bear it.

"Mom lived down there with me when I was a baby. Or so she says. Then she stopped." Paul sighs. "Seven years later, she got pregnant again. I guess that's when Father decided she had to give birth in a hospital this time so that he could swap the babies if there was anything wrong."

"I guess so," Mark says quietly. "Wow, our parents were fucked-up."

"But we're not," Paul says brightly. "At least, not too much."

"Speak for yourselves," I say. "I think I am."

Paul laughs, and hearing it feels healing.

"What happened after you were found?" I ask.

"The police couldn't get anything out of me. I was mute." He shrugs. "I faked it for a few months. It was the only thing I could think of to stop them learning where I came from. I'm sorry, little brother, but I didn't want Mom arrested. I still loved her."

Mark just nods.

"Anyway, they checked me over at the hospital and figured out that I have Treacher Collins. I had some sight and hearing issues. Plus, I was malnourished and underdeveloped. I stayed in the hospital for a little while, then I was adopted." He stands, grabs another photo from the window, and presents his adoptive family—two smiling parents and a younger sister. "Honestly, from there, I had a very happy life. There were… bumps along the way. Nightmares. Lots of therapy." He laughs. "But I'm still here, and I'm still smiling. And I've written five science fiction novels now. Honestly, I'm not sure my imagination would be this crazy if it hadn't been for the room."

"Did you ever tell anyone?" Mark asks.

"I told my wife," he admits. "But I still haven't told Mom and Dad. They think I may have been abandoned somewhere, but they don't know the full story. Maybe I'll tell them now Catherine and Nicholas are both dead."

"I can't believe she never even looked for you." Mark shakes his head. "She went on as though nothing had happened. I mean, I know she was sad, but she still carried on."

"She was a coward," I say bluntly. "She chose Nicholas over her own flesh and blood."

Paul's expression tightens. "I think you're right. But she'd come down to the basement with bruises on her arms and legs. Mark, I think you were too young to notice at that time."

Mark swallows hard. "I'm sorry, but I can't feel sorry for her."

"That's okay," Paul says. "You don't have to."

"She didn't know how to be grateful for anything," Mark

says. "She only knew how to take what she wanted. Take the easy way out. She ruined lives for what she did."

"I'm sorry you didn't get to grow up with your real parents," Paul says. "But even if we aren't related by blood, I think of you as a brother, and I hope you can, in time, view me the same way."

Mark raises his head, his chin trembling. "I already do."

None of us speaks for several seconds, just letting the weight of the words sink in and restore us to some sort of normalcy, as much as can be had in a situation like this.

I take Mark's hand, cradling it. "We would love to keep you in our lives, and..." I look at Mark, who nods as if it's okay for me to continue, "in our baby's life."

Paul's head snaps up. "Your... baby?"

A grin spreads across my face, and I instinctively touch my stomach, which will soon swell round with the life growing inside it.

"We're expecting. We found out last week."

Paul stands and claps. "Congratulations! That's wonderful!"

We stand, too, exchanging hugs with him.

"We'd love it if our baby called you Uncle one day," Mark says, his eyes red and his lashes damp.

My eyes tear up, too, but through the blur, I can see the joy spreading across Paul's face.

"Oh, I can't wait to tell Taylor," he says. "This is wonderful!"

On impulse, I pull Paul into a hug, finally getting an opportunity to hold the hurt little boy who wrote those diaries in his basement prison. I squeeze him tightly until Paul lets out a laugh and pries himself away.

"Sorry," I say, brushing away tears. "I just can't believe it. I thought I was going to die in that place while I was reading your diaries. And now I'm here, and you're here, and Mark's here, and we can get to know one another. It's a miracle."

"The universe is full of miracles," Paul says. "If you just let your soul be led, it will always find a way to get to them."

The words wrap around me like a gift, and I realize it wasn't just about luck and timing and surviving. It was about *all* of that lining up in all the right ways.

It wasn't my time to die in that room, or Paul's. We still had more to give to this life, more to learn, and more ways to grow as humans who could leave a lasting imprint on the world, to grab the world by the hands and say, "You will not break me. I am unbreakable. I am a survivor."

I keep thinking back to that first day when I thought I saw movement in the attic window. It's like the house was warning me not to stay. The house told me it was haunted, not by ghosts but by evil deeds.

It doesn't matter now. Catherine is gone. She left a lasting shadow on our lives, but we're more than happy to walk in the sun. It won't be easy, but I'm determined not to dwell on any painful memories. I won't let the trauma of my past affect my child's future. Not like Catherine did.

I lean my head against Mark's shoulder and breathe in his familiar scent—soap with a hint of cologne. I'm free. I'm home. I'm growing a tiny human in my body, the miracle of life coming full circle. And that's exactly what it feels like in this moment, the circle of life continuing, being fulfilled, by my little family and the light of new beginnings shining radiantly around all of us.

ABOUT THE AUTHOR

SL Harker was raised on Point Horror books and loves thrills and chills. Now she writes fast-paced, entertaining psychological thrillers.

Stay in touch through her website: https://www.slharker.com/

Join the mailing list to keep up-to-date with new releases and price reductions.

ALSO BY SL HARKER

The New Friend

The Work Retreat

The Bad Parents

The Nanny's Secret

The Secret Family

The Nice Guy

Printed in Great Britain
by Amazon